CUP OF EVIL

E. GROAT

PUBLISHED BY FIDELI PUBLISHING INC.

Published by Fideli Publishing Inc.
119 W. Morgan St.
Martinsville, IN 46151

www.FideliPublishing.com

To my son, Mr. Wonderful.

CHAPTER 1

It was one of those winter nights that promised punishment to anyone fool enough to venture out. Shutters creaked and awnings moaned from the previous night's heavy snowfall, while a wet, raw wind ripped through the gangways between grimy buildings on Western Boulevard in lower Manhattan. It whistled through the carcasses of stripped and forgotten Fords, Plymouths and Metros that populated this frozen industrial wasteland, where buildings had once been moguls of commerce and light industry.

Suddenly, with comic-book vividness, Zoe Erskine appeared, swathed in a crimson cape and wearing a hat trimmed in white ermine. She limped, as she wore only one knee-high, butter-soft boot. Her right foot was almost bare, except for remnants of a shredded nylon stocking, and the cold had turned her rosy-painted toes a fire-engine red.

Zoe was young and graceful, and always moved quickly and lightly. Even she found it difficult to negotiate the snowdrifts and ice patches. Falling once, then twice, she picked herself up and worked her way slowly and deliberately through this hostile landscape, pausing only to glance at her unprotected foot. She was in pain and mildly frightened, unable to focus through tearful eyes caused by the wind and snow. The confusion and despair evaporated when she heard Garth's voice above the quiet hush of the night.

"Zoe! Zoe! Where's the pizza?" he said. "And what the hell happened to you?" The priority of the questions did not go unnoticed. She would think about that later.

"Hush, Garth, gotta tell you..." She spewed the words, breathing heavily as she fell into the car door Garth had just swung open. "First, get me out of this freezing weather, and forget your damned stomach."

Garth wheeled the Mercedes past lost, defenseless souls gathered for warmth in forgotten corners of this almost-deserted part of the city known as the Big Apple. Save for Tiny's Pizza and its infamous ribs, why else would they be in this awful place at midnight? Two blocks uptown in her usual surroundings, she thought little of the seamier side of life. Only when hunger overtook Garth at odd hours of the night was she touched by those less fortunate. After a marathon of lovemaking, Tiny's usually came to mind. Zoe had been with Garth now for more than two years,.

She had known him since she was a kid, when Garth went to work for her father. Warren and Garth were a match made in heaven, both champions of the underdog, good guys fighting for the cause. Zoe, to her dismay, did not always share their passion. Little did she know that was all about to change on this frigid night, as she scurried from a back alley in the black of night, under the yellow glare of city streetlights.

As she rubbed warmth and feeling into her bone-chilled foot, Zoe regained her composure and began her tale. "The little bastard's back there with Lawton."

"Who?" Garth drove on sullen, his hunger denied. "What the hell you talking about anyway, Zoe?"

"Beckman," she raged.

She recalled Beckman making news last week, slobbering all over the aldermen on the city council about what he was going to do with this part of the city. Beckman was chief slumlord and tenement bigwig in these parts, and Lawton was his ordained gofer.

Before his death, Warren A. Erskine had his own plans for the city. Plans far removed from what Beckman had in mind. The rebirth her father had envisioned was one of manufacturing, research, building, and commerce. What this place had once been, it could be again, teaming with the can-do spirit and chances for all hardworking individuals chasing the American dream. This was the place where movers and shakers of a bygone era made things flourish and grow. If Chicago was the big shoulders in Sandburg's prose, then New York was the heart, soul, and mind of the nation. Warren Erskine had seen this great city fall into decay, and his aim was resurrection. He had planned for years, forging a relationship between city fathers and budding industry, acquiring tax credits, grants, donations and investment for this project.

Maybe life had changed so much that it could never be that way again. People were different or, if not different, apathetic. Look at L.A. Who would have thought the heart of California would put itself out of business and tear down the entire city because of unrest, hatred, union greed, and power grabs? Business was fleeing from overregulation fees, taxation, and fraud. Enterprise zones? Government subsidy? What a joke. The children of Israel built the Great Pyramids in less time. Garth and Warren had worked tirelessly with federal, state, and city officials for the past three years to reach some common ground. The small grants, funding, and donations had started to make the herculean endeavor almost seem a reality. Still, Zoe's faith in the system was never as rosy as her father's. His passing made it all seem futile and unimportant to her, but Garth doggedly held onto what he felt was Warren's reason for living those past few years.

Old-fashioned and idealistic ideas might not cut it these days, but seeing Beckman plotting to destroy her father's dream triggered some dormant fuse in Zoe. At this moment, in this filthy alley, her indifference to his project was frozen in time. Zoe became a team player. The grief and sadness dogging her these past months had renewed itself as firm resolve. Western Boulevard was not going to become a belching and burping zone for New York's wine-and-dine set. Not this time, Beckman. Zoe could hear her father calling to her from the recesses of her mind, coupled with a deep, visceral coercing from her very core.

"I won't let it happen. I promise."

CHAPTER 2

Nelson Randolph Beckman IV stood in the dim glow of the security lights that hung from the chain-link fencing enclosing what used to be the James Buchanan School. The light's white glow exposed the final decay of the old school, another victim of inner-city rot. Beckman's eyes, with their perpetual squint, were focused intently on Josh Lawton—his top advisor, attorney, and pimp for any unseemly job that needed to be done.

"Have we got Harris yet?" Beckman bleated. Contrary to the opulence and regal bearing his name implied, he was a weasel of a man with a weaselly little voice. There was no indication of education, heart, or graciousness. For all his money, there was no Harvard background, no polo ponies or yachts berthed on Long Island. He envied all that in a small way, but he had neither the bearing nor the breeding to be really accepted by the social elite of New York. Old money still had a certain caste system, of which Nelson Randolph Beckman would never be a part. They merely tolerated his vulgar little self, for the sake of the bulk of his vulgar little wallet.

Beckman's sole reason for existence was to obtain, control, and win at any cost. In short, Nelson Randolph IV was not a nice man. His only soft spot was a passion for authentic Louis XV furniture, the more ornate the better. His Manhattan penthouse was strewn with the stuff. Wouldn't old Louis be happy to know that most of his earthly treasures had somehow ended up in storage with or surrounding Nellie R. Beckman. There was something very Freudian about this collection of treasure; it put old Louis and Nellie on the same plane, somehow on a first-name basis.

None, save perhaps an old, dead king would refer to Nelson R. Beckman as "Nellie." That moniker was reserved for a chosen few. His ninety-two-year-old mother—whom he loved dearly and catered to unceasingly—and his wife, who was thirty years his junior. He tolerated her; she was simply for show. Nellie, you see, had no attraction for the fairer set. His sexual preference was perverted, to say the least, bordering on cruel and unusual. He liked pain—not his own, but he loved to see it in others. In short, Nelson R. Beckman was just not a nice man; he was an evil one. This fact his mother did not know.

"Well, have we got him or not?" he repeated. Lawton's answer did not come fast enough, and Beckman made a sweeping gesture with his hand to get Lawton's attention.

"Mr. Beckman, I told you last week it was not going to be easy. This mayor-elect Harris, spawned from this so-called special election, is in the tank for a lot of people. He's a bum, a corrupt shyster, a drug user. The people know it and the son-of-a bitch still gets elected. So much for our system; for the people and by the people. The guy's got pull somewhere.

"We have to move slowly," Lawton continued, frustrated. "I haven't got sufficient and strong enough background yet to really do him and his associates in. This one may take more than cash. Don't forget, Erskine and Avery have been working on this proj- ect for three years. They have foreign and domestic interests signed up and ready to move, and most of the funding. Right now, all they need is the blessing of this bum Harris and the city planning commission. Erskine's death and the special election are prob- ably the only things that stopped this project from happening."

"Do it." Beckman whipped his bony finger in Lawton's face one more time. Then he softened his voice and half smiled. "See that it's taken care of by next week, Josh." He motioned to his two associates and vanished out the door.

Joshua W. Lawton breathed easier as he followed in Beckman's wake. Once inside his car, safe from the torment of the elements, he began to contemplate Beckman as he so often did, asking many questions of himself. What in the hell was he doing in a place like this, skulking like a criminal, talking to lowlife scum like Beckman anyway? The answer always came back the same. He was skulking because of Beckman's flair for the dramatic, and what he was doing *was* criminal. The only reason, he mused, was his father. Along with his substantial inheritance and the prestigious law firm his father built, Lawton and Lawton. Beckman was somehow part of his inheritance—something about family obligations, old friendships, and debts that needed to be paid. Beckman's security, and safe passage for his sometimes-unsavory business dealings, was all wrapped up in a promise made to Josh's father before he died. Josh, however, did not fully understand the lengths he had to go to fulfill that promise.

In truth, Joshua Lawton was a good man, honest and loyal. His wealth was achieved by dealing everyone a straight hand, which made it all the more difficult to align himself with Beckman. He despised the man, and Beckman knew it. Yet Beckman also knew he could trust this offspring of the senior Lawton. Josh was like his father, weak in that he considered integrity and truth part of the human condition. Not stupid mind you, just too damn idealistic. All his business dealings were "legitimate," if not moral, just as they were with his father.

Such was the plight of a man of honor with a strong sense of loyalty. God, how Josh wished Beckman would fall off the face of the Earth. Everyone's life would be easier. The only reason Beckman wanted to possess this part of town and destroy reconstruction plans was because he hated Warren Erskine with a vengeance that did not diminish even after his death.

As lousy as Beckman was with his dealings, Erskine was the antithesis of him. His operating mantras had been high credibility, quality work, and business standards—and he aced Beckman every time. Willful spite and jealousy were the only forces driving Beckman, which meant that Erskine's partner Avery and his daughter Zoe had become business prey.

Josh knew them both and respected them, even the project they had planned for this dismal place. After meeting Zoe last year at a fundraiser, he even found himself mildly attracted to the dark-haired, blue-eyed lady. She was charming, intelligent, and very, very resourceful. She had managed to turn a group of notoriously tight-fisted Wall Street barons into willing investors in her father's idea of rebuild and rebirth. Josh was now finding himself caught up in the memory of her very fair, flawless face, framed by sleek, almost-black hair that cascaded loosely about her face. She reminded him of the classic Scarlett in *Gone with the Wind*. This whole thing had become all too ridiculous; it was downright shameful that he had to be the one to prevent her project from seeing daylight because of circumstances beyond his control. A promise made long ago to his father made him an unwilling enemy of Zoe Erskine. He did not feel this was right or fair. She was a lovely foe, but there was unfortunately no way to be on her side of the fence, no matter how noble the cause.

Josh noticed on the dashboard clock that it was three in the morning when he wheeled into his reserved parking space. What a night. He needed some sleep, as he had a meeting with Harry the next day. Harry, a man he had known since his teens, was Josh's eyes and ears. Josh, the upstanding forty-three-year-old lawyer with impeccable credentials, depended greatly on streetwise guys like Harry to achieve the desired outcome in many of his cases. Strange bedfellows indeed. "Did I say bed?" he thought. His apartment key gave no backtalk. He soared through the bedroom door and greeted the four-poster like a new puppy greeting its master with pure joy. He stretched broadly and kicked off his tasseled Allen Edmonds with an abandon unusual for the otherwise-tidy Mr. Lawton. He wriggled out of his hand-tailored Hickey Freeman suit and tossed it aimlessly toward the large wingback chair he used so often for his reading pleasure. Arthur Conan Doyle and Sherlock Holmes seemed to be holding firm this month, and Josh revisited Doyle often. Pulling back the comforter, Josh scurried between the sheets, switched off the lights, and curled his lean, six-foot frame into a fetal position.

CHAPTER 3

In the pre-dawn hours, Garth had just kept driving, letting the miles fall behind them. They had pulled off 95 about a half an hour ago to have a bite to eat at a 24-hour truck stop they had discovered about a year earlier. Garth knew the back roads and high roads around this part of Connecticut pretty well. He and Zoe used to frequent them in the old days, when they first met.

Zoe had finally calmed down after an hour of raging over her discovery of Beckman and Lawton. Garth found himself amused, feeling her wrath toward these two. He never knew that her commitment to this project was quite this strong. He did know, however, that her father's death had a profound effect on Zoe. For the longest time, she had felt that this downtown project was responsible for her father's untimely departure from this good Earth. It was good to know she felt as strongly as he did about Warren's project. Garth had tried to assure her that it was just a matter of time before this all became a reality. Unfortunately, one of Garth's failings was that he was an incurable optimist. Cross all you T's and dot all your I's, work hard—and voila! All you've strived for will come to pass. Sometimes his unfailing optimism and good cheer drove Zoe over the edge.

The past three-plus years had not been easy. After Warren had surveyed this downtown area and started thinking these wretched avenues could be viable again, he contacted Garth—construction engineer, small-time developer, and entrepreneur. Garth had done work for Warren before, and their association had become long and profitable. Garth respected him and, by the end, loved him as he did his own father. But, he never realized he'd be so completely sucked into Warren's dream. After several meetings in abandoned, skeletal remains of brick and mortar, Garth found himself shaking Warren Erskine's firm, outstretched hand. He never looked back. They were partners, and in the ten years he had known Warren, he had never let him down. Not even in death. There was a substantial business-insurance policy in Garth's name, which Warren had taken out the year before he died. Garth discovered this while going through the normal business documents. There was a large envelope with Garth's name scribbled in Warren's handwriting, and the policy provided well for him and the business. Garth was hell bent to see this project through. Beckman or no Beckman.

Garth looked over at Zoe, who was now asleep. Earlier, they had decided to go a little farther up the coast to New Haven Harbor. Hell, it was Saturday, and they both needed a reprieve. Garth headed for the cabin where they had first made love.

By the time they reached their destination, the sun was rising in the east. It was a glorious day, so much so that the sun on the snow was blinding. They made their way through undisturbed snowdrifts to the cabin that was about one hundred yards from the road. Once inside, Zoe busied herself uncovering furniture and brewing coffee, making it downright homey. She had been coming there since she was a child, and always felt quite domestic. This was where she and her mother made breakfasts and dinners for friends and family. Her father loved to fish, and would bring his catch of the day to her mother to prepare, always declaring that this catch was bigger and better than the last one. The cabin had several pictures of the family grinning stupidly over a stringer of fish her father proudly held.

Those were the days she fondly remembered. Now she and Garth would make new memories to love and cherish. A roaring fire was all that was needed to make the Christmas-card surroundings complete, and Garth soon provided one by hauling in the well-seasoned hickory and oak stored behind the cabin. This was a small chore for Garth, whose contractor body was muscular and used to hard work. He chose one large oak log, along with several smaller logs and kindling, and soon he had the makings of a first-class fire. Exhausted, Garth made sure the fire was blazing, then eyed the huge, old bed covered with woolen and down blankets. Gathering each other in their arms, he and Zoe hugged each other tightly and went to sleep.

Dreamily, slowly, Garth awoke to soft caresses and to lips sweetly nibbling his earlobe. "Umm…is that you, Mildred?"

The reply came with a sharp jab to the ribs, and a quick twist of the same ear that was relished like chocolate mousse just moments ago. Turning over in mock surprise, he met his assailant. "Oh it's just you," he teased. She attacked him with her only means of weaponry. The goose-down pillow pounded him unmercifully, but Garth—superior fighting man that he was—would not take this lying down. Maneuvering for a frontal attack, he zeroed in on her tiny waist, and brought her down in a sea of giggles. Small and intense, Zoe fought back bravely, but to no avail.

"Turn in your sword," he demanded.

"Never," she said defiantly. "You turn in yours."

He lowered himself to her and kissed her, warmly, deeply. Equally vanquished, he did indeed turn in his sword, his love, his loyalty, and his life. Zoe Erskine was the only woman he would ever love.

They ate dinner that evening in New Haven, after Zoe made a quick shopping trip to replace the boots and stockings she had destroyed by stepping in the sewer grate back in the alley when she was spying on Beckman, as a momentary fear of being caught had made her panic. She wrestled with her foot and was unable to free it, twisting her ankle in the process and having to abandon half of a favorite, obscenely expensive pair of boots. Zoe was well off, but she was always taught to respect a dollar. The loss irked her. It was something else for which Beckman was going to pay.

A big, ugly bruise appearing on her foot and ankle did not improve her mood, as she brooded about the weasel of a slumlord. Garth had picked up a pair of slippers and cotton socks at a gas station to tide her over, but now she chose a pair of gray suede pumps, gray woolen slacks and a white angora turtleneck. She returned to the cabin to find Garth reading an outdated *Smithsonian*. She showered and changed into her new duds, gained Garth's glowing approval, and sped out the door to feast at the local oyster bar. Garth ate slowly, with silent appreciation for every bite; it was the first they had eaten since the diner. Now it was well past seven when they sat down to steak and lobster at The Cove. Overstuffed and content, they had the rest of the night and all day Sunday to relish each other's company.

Garth had managed to put Beckman on the back burner for now, but many of the things Zoe had told him about the conversation between Beckman and Lawton were disturbing. Extortion, graft, blackmail... what else? He would start with the mayor's office on Monday morning.

CHAPTER 4

Harry was late, as usual. He ambled into Josh's office, looking like he fell out of a Dashiell Hammett novel or a classic Bogey film noir. Whatever he did to affect this style, it suited him. When talking to Harry, Josh always conjured up words like "gumshoe," "dame," and "rod." All he needed to complete the visual was a drooping cigarette hanging languidly from his lips, but his doctor demanded he quit last year. He was also cautioned to go easy on the Jack Daniels. It seemed his health had brought him reluctantly into the modern world. He tossed his felt hat and trench coat on the couch, and greeted Josh warmly.

Make no mistake, this "street person" was very refined and polished. His gleaming white shirt punctuated the cut of the navy-blue pinstripe suit, and the light-blue, solid-silk tie accentuated the blue of his eyes and the gray at his temples. He was tall and lean at fifty-three, and his somewhat secretive past seemed to add to his appeal. The smell of government or military surrounded him. What little Josh knew of him was unimportant—he knew that Harry was streetwise, knew things, and had connections. These attributes gave him the ability to get things done. Josh was fresh faced and just out of law school, at a meeting of his lawyer peers, when he met Harry. Statements were made indicating that if any dirty work had to be done, Harry was the man for the cleanup. Josh had used him many times since that first encounter. Harry was another prize he had inherited from his father.

"Got anything for me?" Josh asked.

Harry perched himself on the edge of the desk, withdrew a small leather-bound notebook, and began the report on Mayor James Leon Harris. "Nothing much, just punk kid stuff back in St. Louis, juvenile rap sheet miles long. He uses aliases a lot. Leon James, Harris Leon, J.H. Leon, James Harris. Affiliated with a lot of known criminals, dope, guns, gangs, prostitution—it's all there. Harris is smart; he operates around the edges but nothing indictable. Strictly ya-got-nothin'-on-me-copper stuff.

"He came to New York about a year ago, and got himself elected to city council," Harry continued. "Most say he strong-armed those votes, brought along two thugs with questionable pasts, Townsend and Webster. Harris does have a weakness for cocaine. Now that he can afford it, nothing but the finest grade. He's done it all, Josh. This guy's a low-profile shakedown artist, a pimp, a real sweetheart, and fine upstanding citizen. I swear, Josh, all the crooks are in politics. The ignorant masses elect these guys because they've got the right grin and spew the right buzzwords. There's nothing you can really use for leverage."

"Harry, I need something, and I need it now. Quick and actionable."

"Don't worry, kid," Harry said, "I'm working on it. Should have something for you by next week. We'll get someone to squeal." With that, he picked up his hat and coat and headed for the door. "See ya later, kid."

Strong-armed, sweetheart, squeal! Only Harry could say words like this and get away with it. "Harry," Josh called out. "If you ever use the words G-Man or Tommy gun, you're through."

"Sure thing, kid." Harry grinned and headed out again.

"Oh, and one more thing."

"Yeah, Josh," he crooned.

"How long have I known you now? Sixteen, maybe eighteen years?"

"Uh huh," came the reply.

"What's your last name?"

"Smith," Harry said with a boyish grin. "Gotta go now. Gotta a date with a chicken inspector."

CHAPTER 5

Garth climbed the long, pink granite stairs to the city hall with an air of assurance, as was his nature. Punctuality was also part of his nature, and it irritated him to be kept waiting, even by the mayor. This meeting at nine was set up two weeks ago. Just as the increasingly red hue to his complexion became apparent and his black-Irish temper was about to best him, a large oak-paneled door opened.

"The mayor will see you now, Mr. Avery," a pleasant woman announced, forty-five minutes late.

Garth strode through the door, trying to keep his irritability in check. He had come too far to piss off this new mayor. In the deceased mayor Hanks, Garth had an allied force. This association with Harris was yet to be tested, and Garth had not heard good things about this man. There were rumors and whispers that the guy was an inexperienced asshole, with fingers in every pocket. Certainly not capable of filling Mayor

Hanks's shoes. Garth kept his fingers on the pulse of the city pretty well, through contractors, architects, engineers, and inspectors. If the rumors they told him were accurate, Garth would be dealing with a less-than-honorable character.

"Good morning, Mr. Avery," Harris chortled as Garth extended his hand.

"Good morning, Your Honor. It's good of you to take time to see me."

"Now," said Harris, "What can I do for you?"

"Well, Your Honor, I was expecting that you were aware of the reason I'm here. These past three months, since Mayor Hanks's death and during your transition period, I've been working with your chief counsel, Mr. Townsend."

Harris knew full well why Avery was there. However, he wanted Garth to understand the full impact of working with a different perspective. Harris was not Mayor Hanks.

"It's the downtown project, Your Honor," Garth continued. "The blighted area, six square blocks between Western Boulevard and Longfellow." Garth's answer met with a quizzical stare.

"The land and buildings have been purchased from the owners who still had property there, and the remaining abandoned buildings and land with over-due taxes and liens have been resolved. It's unfortunate, Mayor Harris, that we did not have the opportunity to work with you from the beginning of this project. The original concept, programming, and marketing plan were presented to the city more than three years ago by Warren Erskine. His concept was that this inner-city urban blight could be transformed into a self-sustaining, integrated system, bringing commerce from the surrounding city and nearby areas.

"I'm sure you knew of his reputation as a builder, developer, and philanthropist. I would like you to know, Mayor Harris, that his death has in no way dampened the spirit of this endeavor. All interested parties, myself included, are committed to finishing this project. We have worked very closely with the local Black and Hispanic communities. We have Cuban, European, Asian, and even Saudi interest. We have just spoken to a small leather-goods manufacturer who is showing interest in taking over the old tannery building. These are all small businessmen with very little money to invest, but with great backgrounds, ingenuity, and hard work. Investment..."

"Mr. Avery," Harris interrupted. "Before you go on, let me say this. I have done some checking into this project, and the fact is there are still well over $900,000 in tax liens that have to be satisfied. Surely you must understand, Mr. Avery, that in these days of highly scrutinized politics, I must be very careful about how the city's funds are spent. I am accountable for all collected revenues. Please understand, arrangements that were made between Mr. Erskine and Mayor Hanks have no validity now. This whole thing must be re-evaluated, Mr. Avery."

"But, Mayor Harris," Garth went on, barely keeping his anger in check. "In view of the projected increased revenues and broader tax base for the city, the previous administration was very flexible with its collection policy. Mayor Hanks worked hand in hand with us to augment our efforts to attract new business through the chamber of commerce and public-relations campaigns targeted for this area..."

"Mr. Avery," Harris interrupted again. "I cannot deal with lofty idealism and concepts. We must deal with the facts and figures, and the facts are the city treasury has not been satisfied. I must take all this into consideration before any permits are issued. All these facts must be reassessed. Maybe after further study regarding financial theory and investments, we can come to some kind of working arrangement. Now, I hope you will forgive me, but I do have a busy schedule."

Garth rose from his seated position with clenched teeth, but managed to be civil to Harris. "Yes, Your Honor, we'll be talking soon."

Polite, so polite, Garth knew the son of a bitch had his hand out. He'd been through this too many times, in different situations, not to recognize the signs. And, this was not a chicken-feed mayor, "Over $900,000, I believe he said," Garth thought. "Maybe twenty percent of a multi-million project. We'll see, Mayor, we'll see." Garth headed back to the office to think over this giant bugaboo.

Harris sneered at the air of contempt that Garth had left in his wake. "There are other players now, Mr. Avery," the mayor said to himself. "Let's just see what Beckman has in mind. Anyway it goes, Beckman, Avery, no skin off my nose. Just the best deal for me, gentlemen. The best deal for me." Mayor Harris leaned back in smug assurance, certain the big payoff was within his grasp, no matter which road he traveled.

CHAPTER 6

While Garth was exchanging pleasantries with the mayor, Zoe was across town at the Calhern Gallery, having coffee and croissants with John Calhern. Zoe had hosted a fundraiser last year, and John was kind enough to offer the use of his gallery and services again. Her friendship with John was one of true respect and love. He was another longtime friend of her family, so seeking advice from John came second nature to her. Her father Warren, barrel chested and roughhewn, was the last person one would expect to appreciate a Gainsborough or Raphael, but he loved delicate, fine things like porcelain and potteries—and John was a man her father trusted to school him in the values of fine art.

John Calhern was a self-effacing kind of guy who loved art for art's sake, but he also loved the business of it. He would openly admit to inside circles that most of the stuff in his gallery was "crap." The really good stuff he safely kept secret, showing it only to customers who truly appreciated its value. He just never quite understood the mindset of the wealthy, and why they paid for the "stuff." John looked around his high-tech, ultra-modern surroundings. When he spied Zoe, he motioned her over toward his office, which was tastefully decorated in Old World tradition.

"Ah, you're here to raise money," he said. "We'll do it again as we did last year, only better."

Zoe let John do the talking and planning while she polished off the buttery, warm croissant John had offered her, washing down the last morsel with French-roast coffee from the finest Dresden china.

John's imagination was still soaring as he escorted her out of the office. Casually, out of the corner of his eye, he spied one of his clientele pondering a large, black canvas adorned with red rings signifying *Birth & Death*. John excused himself for a moment, put on his best gallery persona with his nose tilted slightly up, and approached his quarry.

"I see you have been enticed by one of our most powerful pieces. What do you think of it?"

Zoe likened it to a cheetah stalking his prey on *Wild Kingdom*. John sold it on the spot for $6,500, assuring Mr. Hastings that it would be delivered the next day. He strolled back to Zoe, check in hand.

"What can I say?" he sniffed. "The stuff sells. Better than my charcoal renderings at the square in New Orleans." They both chuckled and agreed to meet again on Friday.

Outside, the warmth and brightness of the sun on Zoe's face failed to dislodge the shock of the bitter cold. She thought of John Calhern and his artsy crowd. The thought warmed her. They certainly had been good for the Erskine Fund. There was such a bounce in her step, she didn't feel the need for a taxi. She walked the two blocks to St. Xavier to meet Father Fitzhugh.

The stillness of the shrine overtook her as she stepped in from the shrill noise of the New York street; as always, she was overwhelmed by the sanctity and solitude of the church. She knelt before the Holy Mother and whispered a small prayer, then turned toward Father Mike's small office in the rectory.

"Come in, come in," he boomed.

His many years in New York had failed to abolish his Irish brogue. His huge hands took both of Zoe's warmly in his own.

"Miss Erskine," he frowned playfully. "It's about time you visited your parish priest. Has the Good Lord been taking care of you, or have you been an awful handful for Him?"

"A little bit of both," she said, beaming.

With that, he smiled warmly and escorted her to a rather uncomfortable, high-backed chair. "To what do I owe my being graced by such beauty?"

"Father," she lowered her eyes in feigned surprise, "I just know you have part of the Blarney Stone tucked beneath your pillow at night."

"Could be, Miss Smarty Pants. Now tell me why you are here."

She grinned and told him she was there for two reasons. One, to invite him to her next fundraiser at the Calhern Gallery. And two, to enlist his help with donations for the children's and community center they had planned. St Xavier had outgrown its children's facility years ago, and Father Fitzhugh was anxious to be of help in any way he could. He was well aware of her father's plans for the rehabilitation of the blighted area downtown. Warren had been a member of his parish for the last thirty-five years, a golfing partner, and a confidant. Father Fitzhugh had broken bread with Warren Erskine and his family many times over the years. He had baptized Zoe as a baby, and prayed for her recovery when she had a bout with meningitis as a child.

"Now Zoe," he said. "You know the church is behind you one-hundred percent. You just need to tell me where, how, and when, and I'll be there."

"Oh, and Father Mike, I need to tell you one more thing. I'm asking the same of Rabbi Isserman and Reverend Joyce."

He wriggled his nose in disdain. "Don't you worry about that for one minute. We're all in this together. Now go, get out of here, and let me get some work done."

Zoe hugged him and headed out with one more stop in mind. The old fullback from Notre Dame watched her leave with twinkling eyes. He pledged to all the saints that he would not be outdone by Isserman and Joyce. The competitive old elf sat down and started making calls.

* * *

Zoe took a taxi to the Upper East Side. Her destination was the home of Ms. Rachel Stone, school teacher. She was seventy-three and retired now, but still very much in command. She wielded her lessons like a sword, confident they would all hit their marks. Should a blow from her sword of knowledge fall short of its quarry, she targeted the foe of ignorance again with constancy and patience. All of her students had a deep-seated fondness for her, whether they admitted it or not. They might bellyache about her, but they all knew she would see them graduate with better-than-average grades.

Zoe was particularly fond of her and kept in touch over the years, the way she would with a favorite aunt. Zoe's own mother was gone by her mid-teens, so Ms. Stone helped her through awkward and rocky periods in her young life. Zoe was now trying to convince her to come out of retirement to run the daycare center. It would be fully staffed, and she would be in complete control of the subject matter and courses for the older students.

The doorman announced her, and Zoe was allowed entry. After chatting for about thirty minutes, Zoe knew she had Ms. Stone hooked when she reminded her of how drastically things had changed and how there was a desperate need for teachers of her caliber. Granted, her students would be much younger, but the results required were still the same—a good education, high moral standards, and the ability to discern right from wrong. Ms. Stone was just the lady to accomplish this end.

By the time she left Ms. Stone, Zoe was feeling very good about herself, knowing the outcome of this meeting would be very positive. Ms. Stone was never one to back down from a challenge. Hell, she consistently chased them. Illiteracy and ignorance were the enemies, and she was Genghis Khan.

Ms. Stone was alone. She had been alone as long as Zoe could remember, but she knew there was more to this beautiful, gruffly charming lady. Somewhere down the line, Zoe fancied a great love story gone awry, from which Ms. Stone never recovered. Zoe hailed a cab, pondering love denied. Perplexed, she reasoned that lost love was better left to poets.

She directed the cabbie home to her own true love, anxious to tell him of her productive day, unaware of the outcome of Garth's meeting with the new mayor.

CHAPTER 7

Garth had returned to the office and spent the day going over estimates, drawings, and projections. Over and above his own guys, he contacted all the subcontractors involved, and plotted his course to match the money in escrow. He had no cash flow from other projects, as this one had eaten him up for the past three years. His men were cleaning up odds and ends from previous contracts, but he had taken on no new projects. So if this did not get started soon, he would have to lay off the crews.

He had been so sure they had the green light on this thing. That nagging uneasiness he felt after Mayor Hanks died had turned into a prophetic note. He knew it was wrong never to heed that small voice that whispered in his ear. The bank had gone the limit, while his private money and Zoe's were tied up. The million-dollar insurance policy Warren had left him—though small by industry standards— was his life raft. This he would not touch, even should everything else go belly up.

There was no foreseeable income from this downtown project for the next two years, and the renovation itself would take a year to complete. The figures just didn't work. Ten million, give or take, was his guesstimate, plus the price of the monkey wrench Harris was about to sell him. Enough! He was used up. Leaving his desk in turmoil, he gave a hasty goodnight to Ms. Potter, his assistant of ten years, and headed home to the security of Zoe's arms. They would figure something out.

*   *   *

It looked like a mini-United Nations meeting, but in fact was a coalition of businessmen Warren and Garth had solicited for this project. The group included: a Bavarian chocolatier named Klaus; Moshe, a poor man's Ralph Lauren from Tel Aviv; Ravierez, a Cuban whose family had once owned a tannery specializing in fine leather goods, saddles and bridles; and an African-American businessman named Murphy, who operated two highly profitable specialty wine-and-cheese shops in upper Manhattan.

Murphy had learned his craft by working his way up in the California vineyards. When he returned to New York, he worked in a wine-import shop. Warren met him there, was impressed with his knowledge of wine, and helped him launch his own business several years later. Warren had given a lot of people a leg up. Everyone in the meeting had been touched by him somehow, and they were all counting on the success of this endeavor. A jeweler of Turkish descent, a German machinist, a Frenchman who was a small bottler of spring water and looking to set up shop there...and the list went on. There was Damon, a Greek importer. Hwang Ho, a whiz with computers whose forte was selling, repair, and trade. An attorney named Lou was seated next to Dr. Alverez, a young physician Warren had met in Mexico when he twisted an ankle on a fishing excursion.

Garth smiled to himself, thinking it must be a universal conundrum that doctors and lawyers seemed to seek each other out. The amusing thought left as quickly as it arrived. All in all, there were thirty people there. Garth had called them together to give them a progress report. It was nine on Thursday morning, and Ms. Potter had spent Tuesday and Wednesday tracking down everyone to schedule this meeting. She did very well, and had managed to corral thirty of the thirty-five people to whom Garth had wanted to reveal the progress of their project. The missing five included interior designer Erica Johnson, a furniture manufacturer from Spain named Ortega, dentist John Holliman, dry cleaner Murray Landsing, and the Kuwaiti minister.

This worked out well for Garth's purposes; he wanted a meeting with the minister alone. Garth had forged a relationship with Riza Kamal Pahlevi after the Gulf War, when Warren was awarded contracts for rebuilding many of the ravaged palaces and other government offices. Warren's affiliation with the Kuwaitis actually began with his own father, an engineer who worked for Aramco—one of the world's most valuable companies at that time. Aramco was based in Dharan, and young Warren was brought up in the heady ways and days of oil riggers, gushers, and an occasional marauding tribe. He became a proficient horseman and would ride his grey-roan Arabian from Dharan to the coast. He was like a preferred child to Emir Sabah al-Ahmad, and Warren grew to manhood respecting the way of the Arabs.

They left Dharan when the Brits pulled out in 1961. Kuwait had been a British protectorate since the previous century. Fear of a Turkish takeover was the driving force behind Kuwait's need for English intervention, but by the Sixties Kuwait had no need of outside protection. After his father's death in 1964, Warren continued his relationship with the Kuwaitis, both in the oil fields there and with development in the U.S. Indeed, many of Warren's projects were accomplished because of Kuwaiti investment. Garth had traveled with him to Dharan on several occasions and learned the art of the oil business—from taking it from the Earth on good terms with Mother Nature, to quenching the explosions and fires when she was in a bad mood. A gold pocket watch presented to Warren's father by Sabah al-Ahmad now sat in a teakwood box on Garth's desk, as a reminder of the bond they shared. Warren had placed a high value on that watch, and had given it to Garth shortly before his death. Garth knew then that he loved that man.

Garth tuned out these thoughts, and turned his concentration to the meeting before him. He asked Ms. Potter to schedule an appointment with the minister at his convenience, and schedule the other four early next week if possible. Greeting everyone effusively, he assured them this meeting would not take long. Garth updated them on the progress that had been made in building, funding, security, insurance, and rent structures. He told them groundbreaking was set for spring, but that there were a few setbacks and dollar shortages might take a bit more time to resolve. He felt this was information enough. Going into detail at this time would only distress them, and raise a lot of questions he could not answer.

Garth was brief, and to the point, voicing only positive notes. After a few quick questions and Garth's "Thank you all for coming," the businessmen trailed out of the boardroom in a sea of handshakes and smiles. If nothing else, there was a unity of purpose. Klaus was the last to leave. Before he found his way to the outer door, he stopped at Ms. Potter's desk and withdrew a small box from his great overcoat. For all the world, with his ice-blue twinkling eyes and great mane of white hair, he looked like Sgt. Schultz from the old *Hogan's Heroes* series. The box contained his finest chocolates, filled with liqueurs. "Sweets for the sweet," he said timidly, then tipped his hat, bowed slightly, and almost flew through the door. His old-world mannerisms and courtly charm took Ms. Potter by surprise, bringing a pink glow to her cheeks.

"Why Ms. Potter," Garth cooed. "I didn't know."

"I'll forget you said that, pup," she said as she followed him back into the boardroom. "I was able to get in touch with the minister..."

She was momentarily taken aback when she surveyed the empty coffee cups, half-eaten danish, and napkins strewn about. Informal meeting to be sure! She continued where she left off. "He will only be remaining here for three more days, and said he would be happy to see you this afternoon if you can find the time. He is at the Ritz till four."

"Thanks, Ms. Potter, I'll be there," Garth said. "Oh, and check with Norm to see how he is coming along with the final touches on the Brewster contract. I doubt if I'll be in the rest of the day; hold the fort down for me."

He grabbed his coat and scarf, gave her a peck on the cheek, and was gone. Garth made another fruitless trip to the bank where he and Warren had borrowed so many millions over the years, clutching to the hope that his and Zoe's assets and credit would be enough for the shortages and price-escalating permits he was forced to face. He was not optimistic, but it did not show as he shook the hand of banker John Pierce. Maybe the visit to Riza could be purely social; Garth would hate to put the bite on him again. Sadly, Garth left the bank with the answers he was expecting. Frustration and rejection walked hand and hand this past year. They came to be expected, and needed to be overcome.

$$* \quad * \quad *$$

Garth was greeted with an open-armed embrace from Riza Kamal. His friend's infectious laugh and grand smile immediately made Garth feel better, almost euphoric. He watched as Riza crossed the room in his flowing white aba and his kufiyah trimmed with the gotra. Truly, he was a handsome and exotic figure. His dark eyes invited Garth to be seated at a table filled with edible luxuries, steaming pots of tea, and thick black coffee. Garth appreciated it; he had not eaten since the hasty danish at the morning meeting.

Garth's worries evaporated. He had felt genuinely close to Riza ever since their first meeting, on one of Warren's frequent visits to Kuwait. When the emir summoned them for counsel or contracting, Garth was sent to supervise while Warren stayed back in the States working on his downtown project. Riza and Garth had spent many long hours in 100-degree heat. They had developed a respect for each other, and a camaraderie that was difficult to come by. The afternoon pleasantries wore on, and Garth found himself raising his hand in protest.

"No more, no more, I cannot eat more," Garth said, and belched a complimentary thank you.

Throughout the meal, while speaking of many things, Garth revealed his plight to Riza. He explained the problems he might encounter with the mayor and the fate of the project. Riza had always made him feel welcome and comfortable in uncomfortable circumstances.

The companions, onlookers, and guardians were constants around Riza, and Garth had gotten used to them. With Riza's soft and melodic voice, the urgency of the dilemma did not seem so pressing that afternoon. The minister talked to him as a brother, assuring Garth that everything would work out with this mayor problem. He had come too far and worked too hard to even consider this an obstacle.

In the event that more financing was needed, "Allah will provide," Riza said with a smile. "Now my friend, I must go."

Garth looked at the clock, and saw it was well past five. Ms. Potter had said Riza would be there until four. The afternoon had melted away, and Garth did not feel any of the apprehension or frustration he experienced earlier in the day. He apologized for keeping Riza so late. The response to this was a warm embrace of farewell and a promise that, upon his return, he would contact Garth for a progress report on his investment. With that, Garth took his leave, humming "The Sheik of Araby" in low tones as he left, an annoying habit he could not seem to overcome since first meeting his friend many years ago. Riza had heard him many times, and accepted it as good-natured. Garth hit the streets, practically singing out loud.

The minister's dark eyes narrowed as he watched his friend depart. He had dealt with this kind of problem before, this type of person, and this type of extortion. Money was not the answer, not with dishonorable men like the mayor. Riza knew that Garth Avery was truly a guileless man. Riza Kamal Pahlevi was not.

CHAPTER 8

In the black quiet of the night, Garth reached out for her. Zoe, in turn, responded by cradling his head in her arms. They laid there, quietly listening to the haunting strings of Pablo Casals and scattering terms of endearment in soft, low whispers. He held the curve of her thigh, unable to fully understand the depth of this love. Verses his mother read to him from the Book of Solomon came tumbling to his thoughts, and at this moment the beauty of the words and Zoe's being overpowered every wanton emotion he had ever experienced.

"The hair of thine head like purple, how fair and how pleasant art thou, o love for delights," he recited. "Thou are all fair my love, there is no spot in thee. Set me as a seal upon thine heart, as a seal upon thine arm, for love is strong as death. Or something like that." He squeezed her tightly, sleepily murmuring his feeling.

"Garth, are you okay?"

"You bet. Never felt better in my life, and I've never been more in love with you than this night. Don't know why I'm thinking in biblical terms; maybe I need the wisdom of a Solomon at this stage of our lives. Just trying to say things to you I don't often say."

"Solomon, huh. I'd forgotten how beautiful those psalms were. Let me see..." Into the blackness, cascading from her lips, verses from Solomon swallowed him up. He lay there in awe and astonishment as he listened.

"My beloved is white and ruddy, the chiefest among ten thousand. His head is as the fine gold, his locks are bushy and black as a raven. His eyes are as the eyes of doves, by the rivers of waters, washed with milk and fitly set. His lips like lilies, dropping sweet-smelling myrrh. His hands are as gold rings set with beryl, his belly is as bright ivory overlaid with sapphires. His legs are as pillars of marble, set upon sockets of fine gold, his countenance is as Lebanon, excellent as the cedars. His mouth is most sweet, yea he is altogether lovely. This is my beloved, and this is my friend...Or something close to that," she giggled.

He buried his face into her breasts and kissed them reverently.

"Garth, do you think you're the only one who has these feelings?" Zoe slid down beside him, belly to belly and heart to heart, and they kissed and caressed until the ache of desire washed over them. He mounted her arched torso, and they both found the heavens.

CHAPTER 9

Harry inched his way into the bowels of the beer-and-urine-soaked gathering place known as Rudies. The music and sleazy surroundings repulsed him, but he continued his search for Tommy. Harry found him at the bar, encircled in smoke. The associates he was conversing with departed as quickly as the neon-blue smoke as Harry approached and found a stool next to Tommy. He ordered a Jack Daniels straight up, but did not drink.

Tommy was a tall, lanky sort with horse-like features and a military-like buzz cut. He half smiled and half sneered as Harry approached, and dispensed with any hellos; he knew Harry was not here for a social call. Harry was brief, and the atmosphere was stifling.

"I need your help, Tommy," Harry began. "It's worth ten grand. I need names, uptown names, political, high city. No rumor, proof." The words shot out in quick, rat-a-tat fashion, and Tommy knew right away that Harry must have gotten wind of Mayor Harris's rumored extracurricular activities. Mayor Harris was a relatively new customer around town, and had dealt with a broker who called himself Louis, but Tommy always made it his business to know exactly who he was dealing with. It always paid off, and it looked like his new association with the mayor through Louis was going to be a lucrative one.

"It'll cost you $15,000," he replied. Price of my merchandise has gone up. Health insurance. All my boys and girls have got to have a certificate and a guarantee they're clean, for uptown clientele."

Harry agreed, and threw in an extra $5,000 if he could get it for him within the week.

"Pictures, Tommy. Recordings. Even an article of clothing, cuff link, or jewelry. Something to make it stick."

Tommy understood. He had done this before—not so often as to damage his reputation, but enough when stakes were high. Time for a party, he mused. Tommy threw parties for his merchandise the way Iowa housewives threw celebrations for Tupperware. This one might even interest Lord Beckman. Although Beckman did not do drugs, and he was very discriminating and careful, he was still a high roller who could be induced if the prize was sweet enough. Beckman was also vicious, so much so that most of the boys refused to go back, but Tommy had the right bait this time.

"Hey Tommy." Harry stirred Tommy out of his musings. He issued a short salute, turned, and hastily said he would be in touch.

Tommy returned to his party-planning revelry. What divine coincidence. Sweet profitable Columbian Gold for His Honor Mayor Harris, and two new imports ripe for Nelson R. Beckman's pleasure.

Business concluded, bar bill paid, and so longs noted, Harry gratefully wormed his way to the outside stench of the streets. He passed two obviously infatuated green-haired gents squeezing each other's buttocks and kissing each other feverishly on the dance floor. "Oh jeez," Harry thought. Harry was not a prude; he was just old. There were things he could just never get used to. Male, female, whatever—in his mind, some things just were not meant for public display.

Harry almost fought his way through the final door to the outside world. He breathed deeply, and felt the need to walk two or three blocks just to get things into perspective. Deep down, he knew the world was not always as he perceived it. It just seemed so futile for some. God help those green-haired young people, he thought, drowning in a sea of welfare checks, drugs, and degradation. America's melting pot, filled with nuances of ethnic bouquet and spices, had turned to gruel. Unfortunately, they didn't know it, and no one took the time to tell them there was a sunrise. Anyway, who was he to talk? Ultimately, Harry always managed to end up swimming with the fishes in the same sewer. He made his way through the downtown squalor, whistled for a taxi, and went home. He hoped he wasn't too late to catch the Rush Limbaugh show.

CHAPTER 10

The Calhern Gallery was filled with candlelight and music. John had outdone himself as usual. The fellow who had purchased the obnoxious, $6,500 piece of art just two weeks before was caught up in an equally obnoxious canvas that evening. John was circling, waiting for the proper moment for the kill—but when he saw Zoe arrive, he left his prey in artsy reverie.

"You my dear, put all my works of art to shame." Zoe lowered her lashes in a mock blush and bowed slightly in her best southern belle imitation. "Watch it, Scarlett," John chuckled. "We have a few wealthy feminists here we wouldn't want to offend."

Garth stepped over from a lavishly linen-clad table, and offered Zoe her drink. He shook John's hand warmly and thanked him for all the help he had given their project over the past year.

"Just doing my bit, Garth. Besides, I love doing it. It keeps the pigeons close by and we all feel great about doing something worthwhile."

Zoe scanned the gallery and was thoroughly pleased by the turnout. She gazed down the candlelit buffet filled with succulent culinary treasures of imported cheese, meat, pates and other delicacies. A silver fountain of champagne was cast center stage on the buffet, surrounded by fresh flowers. She noticed Father Fitzhugh close by, his huge hand encircling the fragile champagne ware while he chugged down the golden liquid and mesmerized the ladies with tales from the Emerald Isle. Rabbi Isserman, Reverend Joyce, and their wives were not too far away, embroiled in a discussion of religious warfare and dogma, no doubt enjoying the evening in a less-subdued manner as they drank coffee and hot tea.

All in all, everyone seemed to be enjoying themselves. John always had a knack for turning these things out so they did not seem stuffy. Everyone was happy to give their money, never feeling coerced. Getting people to give, without producing long faces from a feeling of forced benevolence, was a feat few could pull off. John managed to do it quite charmingly. As the evening progressed, Zoe and Garth were caught up in the frivolity of polite conversation and laughter. They even managed to pass the evening without running into the obligatory loudmouth drunk who usually showed up at these affairs. John Calhern ran a tight ship, and would breach no nonsense or disturbance of civility.

However, while Zoe was deep in conversation with Father Fitzhugh, Nelson Beckman appeared with his wife and Joshua Lawton. His appearance imprinted a distasteful pall on Zoe for the rest of the evening. John was escorting them toward her, and she found it too late to escape the meeting once a beaming John began the introductions. Zoe's face paled, and John knew immediately that there was bad blood there. He regretted having brought them over, but Zoe handled it gracefully. She acknowledged the fact that she had met Mr. Lawton at last year's fundraiser, and of course, that she knew of Mr. Beckman since she was a child. When all the polite politics were finished, Zoe excused herself, leaving the Beckmans and Lawton in John's hands.

John soon turned them over to Father Fitzhugh, and followed Zoe to the champagne fountain to request a refill. He didn't know what the problem was, but he was sensitive enough to Zoe that he realized it was not a welcome meeting that he had just arranged. John made this observation known to Zoe, and assured her he would have avoided it had he only known her feelings. Zoe stopped John before he could continue berating himself. How could he have known that Lawton and Beckman were doing everything they could to keep her father's dream from becoming a reality?

"This is a wonderful evening, John," Zoe explained. "Don't think or feel for one moment that you have done anything to spoil it for me. You are the best. This whole thing will work itself out. Don't trouble yourself about this for one minute, promise?" He smiled and nodded. "Now, don't you think it's time for the presentations?"

John called for everyone's attention, and made his way to the small podium he had set up for this special occasion. His introductions were brief, with a general overview of why they were there—for the inner-city revitalization project, specifically the children's center and school, and low-cost housing.

"I am pleased and honored to introduce..." he continued. One by one, eight donors came to the fore with checks in hand, beaming with charity—and some beaming with just a bit too much of the grape. Isserman and Joyce proudly presented the checks from their respective church and synagogue, totaling just under $6,000.

Father Mike followed. His mischievous blue eyes twinkled with delight as he pulled his formidable frame perfectly erect, and in a military cadence announced that St. Xavier had raised $14,492—an almost-impossible task in two weeks. A great round of applause rose from the ranks, and Father Mike's chest heaved. He was in his glory, not unlike when he was scoring touchdowns back at Notre Dame. It was just in him to be the best he possibly could be. Zoe rushed to the podium, encircled his broad chest in her arms, pulled him down to kiss his bald head, and proclaimed to all that the spell of the Blarney Stone must be working overtime for him to have collected this much in such a short time. One more round of applause, and Father Fitzhugh reluctantly left the limelight to join Isserman and Joyce. He acknowledged them with a coy smile and a slight sniff, as he sat down beside them for the remainder of the presentation.

The evening was winding down when a voice from the audience gained attention with one more donation. It was Josh Lawton, who raised his hand and announced a check written for $10,000. On one condition—that he present it to the gracious lady who was behind this benefit, Ms. Zoe Erskine. Under normal circumstances, Josh would not have been so obvious about donations for worthy causes. This spectacle had two purposes. One, to send a loud-and-clear message to Beckman that he was unhappy with the position that had been forced upon him. And two, to let Zoe Erskine know that he supported her cause. Beckman was making the rounds, spreading innuendo and doubt, trumpeting his misgivings that this downtown project would probably never see the light of day. So, in the face of all this, Josh made the donation. While Beckman shot him a deadly glare when the proposal was heard, Josh simply smiled back at Beckman and tipped his glass in response.

All heads turned toward Zoe. The puzzled look on her face indicated she had not yet found the owner of the voice in the crowd. As she followed its direction, her eyes became transfixed when they fell upon the brow of Joshua Lawton. Within moments, she found herself being escorted to the podium by John and Father Mike. By this time, Garth was unsure about anything that was happening during the night's festivities.

Josh and Zoe met eye to eye in front of the crowded room, and she wrestled with the uncomfortable situation with a labored smile and forced graciousness. Josh's presentation of the check was leveraged with yet another condition—it would double if Ms. Erskine had dinner with him the following evening. Anger was erupting in her clear blue eyes but she quickly checked it, like a child retrieving his fingers from the cookie jar when caught. Ensnared by all the eyes upon her and the sizable amount of the check, Zoe acquiesced. This was like a bad movie that couldn't be over quickly enough. Josh extended his hand and she accepted, publicly promising that there would be dinner the next night promptly at eight, at the new bistro called Rembrandts.

The evening was unquestionably very profitable and successful. John deserved a twenty-one-gun salute. But as they taxied home, Garth's sleepy head on her shoulder, Zoe made a mental note. Next time, she must remember to check the guest list before sending out the invitations.

CHAPTER 11

After nursing an absolutely horrible hangover the next morning, arising early, and attending to the awful aches of his mind and body with aspirin and Pepto, Garth returned to the blessed relief of the bed. It was not until well after two that he became acutely aware of the events of the night before, and unable to control his anger over this set-up dinner date. He had not experienced a hangover of this magnitude since he had been a young hard hat working I-beams on high rises. Usually, they were brought on by youthful bets and dares.

The stress of the past several weeks was probably taking its toll. He had been faced with deadlines and layoffs before, but extortion and rigged business dealings were something he could walk away from. Garth had simply said "no" and retreated from insinuations of lower-grade steel or honeycombed concrete. For a field rife with graft in the state of New York, Garth had managed to keep his nose clean and make a decent living playing by the rules. In fact, his high standards and quality control were what initiated his long association with Warren. He wished desperately now that he was here. This mayor thing was something from which he could not retreat, go around, or walk away. Mayor Harris was an obstacle who had to be dealt with; there were too many lives involved. He had to deal with this head on, and this stress no doubt had some bearing on his unusual overindulgence the previous night.

Zoe was not necessarily sympathetic, but she was tolerant. She made him scrambled eggs and dry toast about mid-afternoon, while he sulked about her upcoming dinner with Lawton. He ate his food like a petulant child, feeling too bad to get overly vocal about his feelings.

"Let's let the subject rest now," she said. "It's done, I'll be home early."

Dissatisfied as she was about the situation, she found herself drawn to the meeting with Josh Lawton. For the $10,000 price tag, she could afford a few minutes of her time. Besides, she was curious as to what made this Lawton tick, and what the miserable bastard was up to regarding the downtown project. Zoe viewed this dinner as a trip to the dentist—an unwelcome, but necessary, visit.

Dry toast and eggs did take the wooziness away, and the rest of the afternoon was uneventful. Garth had gotten over his petulant mood, and by six he was actually feeling pretty good. His carping at Zoe had been reduced to a titter, and by the time she was readying herself for the dinner, the tittering had just turned into well-meaning words of caution.

"It is a fact of life," Garth said. "Lawyers are known for being greedy and deceitful, up to no good. Be careful what you say, Zoe. This guy is going to be looking for anything to prevent the project going forward, don't give him a chance. He's going to be looking for a weak spot."

* * *

The fact was, Josh had no idea Garth and Zoe were even aware of his adversarial part in connection with the project. In truth, he simply wanted some time with this lady he found so attractive. That, plus the fact it must have irked Beckman to his very soul. Josh unintentionally found himself grinning back at the mirror as he relished the look on Beckman's face the night before. He made a final inspection of his appearance in the hall mirror, straightened his tie, and continued his gleeful mode on the way to the restaurant. Garth, in the meantime, had settled in for the evening with the new Stephen King novel, and waited for Zoe's return like a fretful father.

Zoe arrived promptly at eight and was shown directly to Josh's table. She wore a rather simple, white, tailored outfit, suitable for professional or evening wear. Rather sizable diamond ear studs managed to enhance the evening effect. Josh rose as she advanced toward the table and extended his hand.

Her gait was aloof, and she touched his outstretched hand like she was handling spoiled meat.

"Whoa, Ms. Erskine, I was hoping this evening would be pleasant for you," Josh said. "Is my presence really that difficult to abide?"

The waiter held her chair so she could be seated, then—with pre-instruction from Josh—disappeared and returned with Rembrandt's finest wine. After obligatory testing of the wine, Josh nodded his approval and the waiter poured for Zoe, and then Josh. Zoe sat there coldly while Josh continued to talk. He announced that he had taken the liberty to order for them, and continued on with explanation that he knew the owner and chef. He had become Josh's client and then his friend, and finally Josh became an investor in the place. Since its opening three months ago, it had done quite well.

Zoe's countenance remained stoic and she finally said quite tersely, "Mr. Lawton, I have no interest in your friends or your investments, or any more of your small talk. Perhaps you will tell me why I am here."

Josh was a quick study, and it didn't take him long to know this evening was not going to be pleasant. "Ms. Erskine," he said, all levity drained from his voice, "I simply wanted to spend a pleasant evening over dinner with a lovely woman, and tell her what a wonderful thing I think she is trying to accomplish."

"Oh God! What a crock!" She did not say these words openly, but her face clearly registered that she thought this man was full of crap. She finally gained enough composure to speak.

"I saw you. I saw you there." This abrupt sentence from her lips did not compute, and Josh awkwardly listened, unable to make any sense out of the words.

"Ms. Erskine, you saw me? Saw me where?" His demeanor was one of complete bafflement.

"You are a two-faced bastard."

Heads turned on this one, and there also seemed to be a slight shimmy in the chandelier.

"Quiet." Josh took her sternly by the arm and reprimanded her for her bad manner. In a quieter tone, he then said, "Now, just tell me where you saw me, and why you think I'm not of proper parentage."

"Western Boulevard, the old school building near Tiny's, early in the morning," she hissed at him.

Perplexed, Josh thought about it for a moment, then said, "What the hell were you doing out there at that time of the morning? It was freezing."

"It's not important why I was there Mr. Lawton; I know why you were there."

"Do you?"

"Yes. I know Beckman has wanted that area, specifically the two blocks surrounding Tiny's, ever since my father laid his plans on the table for Mayor Hanks. But I didn't know what a criminal he really was, or that I would be having dinner with his accomplice and flunky."

"For whatever reason you were out there, Ms. Erskine, did it ever occur to you that things are not always as they appear? I am Beckman's attorney, and only his attorney. This does not mean that I agree with or condone his business dealings, or am anywhere near liking this man. One of the reasons that I'm here tonight is that all the time you were receiving applause and hurrahs for your work, Beckman was working the room doing everything he could do to rain on your parade. Making noises that the project would be deep-sixed before it ever got off the ground. I do not want that to happen, but I won't make any apologies for being at the old school. It's true, I'm technically on the other side of the fence, so professionally I have to do what I can to prevent you from doing what I personally believe is right. Do you understand that? Maybe this will raise the old man's hackles enough for him to dismiss me."

Zoe soaked all this in, but wasn't buying it. She studied his explanation and questioned him with caution, looking for trust like a stray dog approaching a man with his hand held out.

"It's apparent, Mr. Lawton, that you are very well fixed and successful. Why not just refuse his patronage with your firm? What he's asking of you is illegal; I think it's called extortion."

"You heard a lot, didn't you?" he mused, continuing. "At my father's death, when I inherited the firm and its clientele, Beckman was part of it. I've known him since I was a child. I didn't like him then and I don't like him now, but I made a promise to my father that I would serve and protect Beckman, just as he did. So you see, I have no allegiance to Beckman, Ms. Erskine, only the promise I made to my father. My father was very adamant about this, something about an obligation my family had to the Beckman family. It goes back many years."

"It must be one hell of a marker."

"You would think that over all the years my father worked with him, he would have paid his dues. Someday, I hope to find out what it is Beckman hung around my father's neck like a millstone. So please believe me, Ms. Erskine, when I tell you there is no fealty or warmth to Beckman. Only a son's promise to a dying man. This, of course, is none of your business and it is beyond me why I even offered an explanation."

After digesting all this and appraising the sincerity of the man, Zoe softened. In her heart, she felt he was telling the truth. A promise to a father was something she could also relate to, given the feelings she had for her own. She knew how leverage worked in some families. Josh saw her expression change to a more receptive demeanor. Feeling he was on surer footing, he asked, "Can we eat now, and talk about extortion and moral perpetuity at a later date?"

With that, she smiled hesitantly, and Josh summoned the waiter.

CHAPTER 12

Well, Tommy called it right. Beckman did show up, after the invitation and announcement of the particular delicacy that was delivered by Tommy's contact. Nellie felt the offer was too good to pass up, even at the preposterous price Tommy had put on the boy's head.

Needless to say, Tommy knew his clientele, even if they didn't know him. In Tommy's trade, it was always best not to be known directly. His import-export business was just a front for what some had come to believe extinct. Slavery was indeed alive and well, and living in these United States. Civil unrest and war in third-world nations was a boon for lowlife scum like Tommy. Parents seeking protection for their children were eager for them to be sent to America, which they thought was a safe haven. Tommy had acquired these two babies and an older brother from Romania, shortly after Ceausescu and his wife were executed. They were orphaned and half-starved upon arrival. Tommy took them under his wing, and saw to their "well-being." The older boy now, fifteen or sixteen, was virtually left for dead in the street, as some did not adapt well to their new lifestyle in America. In the business of human commodity, breakage of this sort was not insurable or tax deductible.

Tommy always provided lush surroundings for his clientele—caviar and candlelight, so to speak. Mayor James Leon Harris was enjoying life's baser pleasures in one private room. Meanwhile, Beckman indulged himself in a lower level, private, soundproof, and safety locked room where his "social gathering" was being held.

All Tommy's parties were exclusive, but seldom did his guests socialize over drinks and pate. Any fraternization Tommy had with them was strictly cash up front. A fantasy island for all those willing to pay. Tommy tailored the experience to each individual's taste and eccentricities. Now, Mayor Harris? His taste was more conventional than Beckman's, even boring. Harris preferred jazz accompanied by women of all sizes, shapes, and colors. His chosen drug was cocaine, and only the finest. The chosen mood, invincibility. Tonight he had it all, video enhanced.

Mayor Harris's acceptance of the good life, and his misguided idea that he had everything under control, was about to be tested. It was human nature that the most likely cause of a slipup was an inability to grasp reality. Smugness, laziness, lasciviousness, and greed had brought down many a man. Pitfalls abounded, and if Mayor Harris was not careful, he was about to find himself swallowed up by a crater. The wise man who said it was best to learn from other's mistakes had Mayor Harris and his ilk in mind.

While the mayor partook of morally abject pleasure and carnal knowledge, tempting fate to the fullest, the cameras were rolling. How stupid can one get?

CHAPTER 13

A great epiphany overtook Zoe that evening. She had never learned a more significant lesson about not judging a book by its cover. Josh Lawton, after one meal and an evening of conversation, had made her a convert. She found herself a believer in the goodness of this man, convinced that his association with Beckman was only one of loyalty to a promise made to a dead man. She had pursued the discussion of Beckman. However, it was discretionary. Josh would not elaborate on his association with him, as it was not good business practice or ethics. He pointed this out to Zoe several times throughout the evening, and he finally managed to drop the subject by firmly stating he would not discuss Beckman further even if he must leave, no matter how lovely a dinner companion Zoe was. Taking this in good spirits, she vowed never to bring up his awful name again. From there, the subject turned to one another—likes, dislikes, plans for the future, favorite pastimes, and interests. When the evening was spent, one truly transformed lady left the restaurant, as did one very satisfied gentleman, convinced that his initial attraction was one of substance.

Zoe returned home before midnight to find Garth asleep on the couch, remote in hand the television silently hawking some product on an infomercial. It looked like all monsters had been dispatched, as there was no longer a marker in the Stephen King novel. Garth loved King, and all his bogeymen. It would be a pleasure to report that one more demon had been exorcised in the form of Josh Lawton. Leaving Garth's sleep uninterrupted, she covered and kissed him. Sleep came easily to Zoe that night.

* * *

Josh was elated, and unable to sleep. He contemplated the evening, the woman, and the downtown project she was so clearly committed to, and was confronted with a monumental truth. He wanted Zoe and Garth to pull it off, and did not want to be obstacle to what was so obviously a noble cause.

"To hell with Beckman! What is this mysterious thing that ties me to this man?" These questions had gnawed at him before, of course, but they were simply fueled by aggravation, dislike, and frustration with the man. He never had a purpose for examining the validity of the questions. He had known Beckman since he was a child, as he had been one of his father's clients for as long as Josh could remember. Beckman would sometimes join the family get-togethers and dinners. Josh had always abided Beckman's wishes, and saw him through a number of questionable business arrangements, but ignored the tawdriness of them because of his promise.

Now he felt a right-and-wrong turmoil within himself because of this connection he felt toward Zoe and her commitment to this downtown project as a testament to her father. Would he not want the same for his own family? Obviously, the elder Erskine had a higher calling in mind than Beckman did for those burned-out and broken-down buildings. Josh made a decision. He had not seen his mother for several weeks, and it was about time for a visit. Maybe she could explain this family obligation from so many years ago. It was already early morning. He would take a quick nap, and make the hour-and-a-half drive to Suffolk County.

Josh's mother Rachel lived in a well-appointed home. Not one of the great mansions the North Shore was known for, but nevertheless quite acceptable for the area. It was a 4500-square-foot English Tudor on a five-acre parcel. She lived by herself, but had help three times a week. When Josh phoned ahead, she was happy it was Susan's day off, for she looked forward to making his favorite breakfast of three eggs over easy, rye toast, and bacon.

The big house came alive when her children were there, especially around the holidays. That was one of the main reasons she kept it. Josh had an older brother and two sisters, so she never found herself too lonely. Some of the kids and grandkids were always there visiting. Josh was the only bachelor of her brood. When he came to the door, she hugged him tightly and scolded him for not coming up sooner, then led him straight to the kitchen.

After polishing off three rashers of bacon, two patties of sausage, three eggs, and four dollar –sized pancakes, Josh was ready for a snooze. But over his third cup of coffee, he finally got to the point of his visit. His mother was unprepared for this purpose, and therefore took a few moments to think things through when asked about Beckman and her husband's rather shady alliance to him. She was hoping the past would never affect her children. The association did of course come up before, but usually in a casual manner easily dismissed by one of the parents.

This time the question was focused, not to be misdirected or ignored. Josh was intent, and from his demeanor, would not be put off. Finally, she took a deep breath and began. It was not a long story, just painful, but one she was later glad to have finally told.

"Your father was an Englishman in German-occupied Austria, married to Jewess. Me. It was very difficult in those times, your father and I being together, shunned by both sides. We were very young, and I was pregnant with your brother Paul. During the occupation, I was not so lucky. Like millions of others, I was separated from your father, and destined for one of the camps. Just that simple—taken away in the middle of the day with no word by soldiers, while I was waiting for your father in a small café. We had failed to see the signs as Hitler's continued stronghold over Germany and Europe tightened. It was too late for us. The German Reich had closed in, and there was no way out.

"Nelson Beckman and your father were schoolmates and later had a small business association. Beckman was always the young entrepreneur, even in Germany at that time. His father was a high-ranking German official who managed to save me from the camps. I was torn from two sisters and my mother, literally, as we stood in front of a boxcar for shipment."

Josh saw his mother's face grow ashen as she hesitated, but she continued. "Through Beckman's assistance, we migrated to the States. Beckman assured us he would be contacting us for assistance when he was in need. Young Beckman did see the writing on the wall for Hitler. That's it, end of story."

Rachel's unfolding of that time period was short. She was unable to fully relay the horrors she had known. "Shortly after we reached New York, your brother Paul was born, the first of the Lawtons to be born an American citizen."

Josh digested all this. It was surreal, so far removed from anything he had ever known. He had always lived in a cocoon of love, warmth, and security. His mind was playing old movies from his childhood. Nazi storm troopers, Gestapo, searching trains and basements, rooting out Jews in bombed-out buildings where fire and smoke mixed in the blackness of night. Gary Cooper, Marlene Dietrich, Franchot Tone. Those were actors, but this was real. His mind reeled in black-and-white slow motion. His mother poured him a fresh cup of coffee, disturbing his thought process. He looked up at her, beautiful at sixty-eight. Josh arose from his chair and hugged her for a long time, never to fully understand the life she had been through.

She disengaged herself from him and said in a matter-of-fact fashion, "It was a lifetime ago, in another world. It was something your father and I thought not necessary to discuss with our children. Life has been good to us for many years. As for Beckman, he came over shortly after the war, looked us up, and used his favor to your father as leverage. Very subtle, but useful to him. There is no doubt he did save our lives. Your father hated Beckman too, but dealt with him out of pure gratitude. You do what you have to, son. After almost fifty years, it should not fall on your shoulders. It was unfair of your father to ask it of you."

"Well Josh," he thought, "you got what you came for." He hugged and kissed his mother gently as she walked him to the door. As the door opened, he pulled his coat around him. There was still a dampness and chill in the March air, he thought, but perhaps it was the story his mother had just told him that made him shudder. At any rate, he would be glad when spring came.

As he stepped into the car, his mother called out, "We'll never speak of this again, Josh." Joshua Willard Lawton turned toward her and nodded his accord.

CHAPTER 14

The night fell fast and hard for Mayor James Harris. He was fitful and clammy, unable to sleep, and his skin crawled. It may have been the result of overindulgence the previous night, but this was a first for him. He felt eyes on him from every direction. The hasty note from his wife announcing a visit to her mother unnerved him. He was directed not to call, as she needed some time to herself and would talk to him by week's end. Maybe she was getting wise to all his midnight shenanigans; maybe he should tone it down. After all, he needed a faithful and loving wife for his new office of mayor.

"Maybe, maybe, maybe I should blow her head off for treating me like this," he thought. "The bitch knows my position."

It was one in the morning, but he had yet to register one wink of sleep, and those eyes kept following him. He paced fretfully to the living room and poured himself a Courvoisier.

"Ah..." he said as he checked the clarity and deep, rich color in the glass. "White man's drink. Sure as hell beats drinkin' Thunderbird back in St. Louis on Goodfellow Avenue." He positioned himself deep in a comfortable chair and turned on his music of choice. Sweet and low jazz.

Those eyes, damn those eyes—he kept feeling he was being watched. As he laid back and dozed, beads of sweat popped out on his forehead. One...two...three, the sweat slowly trickled down to the corners of his eyes. It trickled down his armpits, and down the small of his back. He was bathed in it now. He awoke to a knife at his throat.

"Lord, Lord, ain't no nigger ever had a knife that big!" he thought in his terror. "Bugs, oh my God, big bugs! Lord! Bugs, my black ass! Scorpions!"

Sweat poured over him. His nose, ears, and upper lip glistened with the stuff in the softly lit room. Black hands, black faces, black eyes peering through black coverings, now whirling about him.

"Still, I must stay still," he thought. "Black-covered faces to whirl with those eyes. My God, those black eyes." Bodies swathed in black sheets were coming at him now. He must breathe, must move, breathe. A silent scream engulfed his being, and he swooned to deep, dark places.

He awoke, and it was not a nightmare. It was fear—deep, raw, black-eyed fear. And when the morning came, his instructions were clear. With his hand trembling, he read the letter, which was finely scrolled in bold print on heavy vellum paper. He reread it three times before the realization set in as to whom the letter was referring: *The path must be made clear for Garth Avery, Mr. Harris. Do we understand each other?*

"Well, hell yes, Mr. Avery. Anything for you." Harris said it loud enough for anyone to hear. He would throw rose petals in his path, accompanied by a brass band, if that's what Avery wanted. He nervously peered around the room. When he heard no response, he ran up the stairs to the shower. He could not help but notice his own stench.

* * *

Minister Riza Kamal Pahlevi was back in town. He slept well that night. He always slept well, assured that many of life's little problems were resolved. Praise be to Allah, and to mankind's resourcefulness.

CHAPTER 15

Tommy made the fifteen grand, as he had proof for Harry before the week was out. He had Harris on video, doing all sorts of things little boys shouldn't be doing, plus an initialed muffler that belonged to Harris. He was so high on coke, he wouldn't have missed his feet. After leaving word for Harry to meet him at Rudies later that evening with cash, Tommy ran a few errands and made copies of the videos at his own home studio. Tommy had all the bells and whistles—the latest in surveillance, recording, photography, and lighting. Tommy took no chances, lest any of his merchandise fall into the wrong hands. There were no subcontractors for Tommy; he did it all. He kept his own library of copies, both to keep any situation under control and for his own personal pleasure.

Harry showed around ten-thirty, made his way to the bar as he did the week before, and found Tommy.

Brief greetings were spoken, and the exchange was made.

"If that's not what you need, let me know," Tommy said. He never stiffed any of his contacts or clientele. They always got what they paid for. An exchange of glances said the obvious—Mayor Harris's goose was cooked politically should these videos end up in the wrong hands. The next morning, Josh Lawton would have the leverage Beckman needed to bring about the end of the downtown project.

Harry cocked his ear to the offending music in the background, looked at Tommy, and suggested that next time they find a new meeting place.

"Personally," Harry grumbled, "I prefer Sinatra."

He stuffed the large brown envelope under his arm, and was gone. Deeply breathing the night air, Harry reflected on what a stinking job this was, to hold a man's life and career in his hands. Well, it was obscene, but he deserved it. Harry took comfort in this observation, even pleasure when he thought about what a sleazeball Mayor Harris really was. His conscience exonerated, Harry hailed a cab, secure in the fact his job was complete.

CHAPTER 16

"My God! My God! My God!" With eyes wide open, Josh's face blanched. "Turn it back. Turn it back."

He was referring to the video that Harry had just played him. Harry had arrived at Josh's office about eight, and they both settled back with Starbucks espresso and jelly doughnuts that Harry brought for the viewing of this first-run edition.

"Stop it there." Josh's eyes became riveted on a figure early in the video. "Harry, do you know who that is?"

Looking closely, Harry answered in his laconic way. "Yeah, Josh. Mr. Slumlord USA. A baby froze to death in one of his buildings a couple of winters ago, remember?"

"Yes, Harry, I remember. I represented him. He walked, because we proved the mother's neglect."

The appearance of Beckman on this video was purely coincidental. Tommy always filmed the arrival of his guest on any given day, as they arrived at their appointed times and were escorted to their designated rooms. On this particular day, Tommy had three individuals invited to one of his little shindigs. Beckman, Harris, and a visiting corporate executive from Houston. The video showed the arrivals of all three, and then the monitor switched to their individual rooms. So essentially, there were three different videos on the same day, with the same beginning. Josh was dumbfounded to see Beckman at the beginning of this one.

"Does your friend have any more on Beckman?" Josh asked. "Can you get a hold of it?"

Harry seemed a bit perplexed. "Well yeah, sure. I think so Josh, but isn't Harris the guy you're interested in?"

"Yes Harry, you got it right. It's just that I'm interested in Beckman as much as Harris, if not more. Go on, play the rest." The video was no surprise to either of these men; they had both seen this type of thing before. Harris did not disappoint. There was enough to wreck a man's life, career, and marriage.

When the recording had ended, Josh picked up the conversation about Beckman's activities.

"Do you know what this is gonna cost you, Josh?" Harry asked. "You are already in over twenty g's, plus expenses and fees. How far do you want to go with this thing? My contact is good, and since you're footing the bill, you know he's not cheap."

"What the hell, Harry, go the distance. I think I have a lot at stake here. Besides, I'm not a cheap pettifogger to be dallied with." Josh was feeling euphoric after the discovery of Beckman on video; it could mean a lot to him. After all these years, perhaps it was Beckman's turn to be beholden. Or he could just call it even and have Beckman out of his life.

"Okay Josh, I'll see what I can do. I'll try and get back to you before the day is out."

"Hey Harry, when was the last time you and I had a drink together?"

"Long time."

"You up for a good dinner tonight? Say Rembrandts? I'm buying."

"Look Josh, I've given up drinking and smoking, not good eating. That means I'm not into haute cuisine at any French restaurant. How about a steak at Perry's, and you're still buying?"

"Good enough, meet you there at seven. I'm depending on you to have that video by tonight, no matter what the cost."

"If I need cash?"

"Same as always, call Sandy at the bank, and your money will be there. See you at seven."

Harry hastened out the door, contemplating the word "pettifogger."

CHAPTER 17

Nothing dampened Josh's spirits the rest of the day, as he sailed through work that had piled up over the past two weeks. By the end of the day, his desk was clear and he was looking forward to the evening, hoping Harry's day had gone as well as his had.

Harry's day, however, had not gone as easily. Finding Tommy in broad daylight was not an easy task. His search came to an end about four, when he located him in a cavernous, dark club somewhere in Times Square—a place where he had initially met Tommy several years back. Then, as now, he was in the middle of some "big deal."

The club was closed, but several knocks—and the mention of certain names—gained Harry entrance. Harry nodded acknowledgment to all surrounding the table, excused himself, and asked for a moment of Tommy's time.

Surprised, and a bit peeved at the interruption, Tommy moved toward Harry and the door for privacy.

"Listen, Tommy, the tape you gave me..."

"What, it's not what you wanted?" Tommy retorted, perturbed. It was rare that any of his work was ever questioned.

"No, no, that's not it. The other guy, at the beginning of the video..."

"Which one?"

"The little toad-faced one."

"Beckman?"

"Yeah, that's him. It's worth $20,000 to me. You got anything on him, I need it by tonight."

The reassuring thought of cash replaced any irritability in Tommy's face. He turned to his compatriots, gave them a nod, and said they would finish up tomorrow. He grabbed his coat and told Harry to give him a couple of hours—and also that it would cost an extra $2,500 for breaking up this little party.

"Don't push it, Tommy," Harry replied. "There are other sources."

Tommy heaved his shoulders and said, "Can't blame a guy for trying." Outside, Tommy directed Harry to meet him at Rudies at six, and he would have what Harry wanted. Harry had just enough time left to get to the bank; he never had an open line of credit with Tommy.

Mercifully, the exchange was done quickly that night. Rudies was quiet at the time, the staff still mopping up from the previous night's crowd, so Harry had no trouble getting in and out. Quickly stuffing the $20,000 in his shirt without counting it, Tommy peered around the hollow, empty room. He always seemed to be nervous doing business in the daylight. Harry noticed the corners of his mouth slightly turn up as he patted his shirt pocket. No wonder—the grinning bastard just collected $20,000 for a few hours of sewer work. Now the snake could crawl back in his hole until next time. Oh yes, the business of sleaze could be very, very lucrative.

Trying to find justification in the simple act of the exchange, Harry left the place bewildered, glad the day was just about over. He entered Perry's with a look of relief. The smell of aged beef, sawdust, and beer on tap reassured him that life was good and all had returned to normalcy.

He spotted Josh hoisting one at a table close to the bar, grabbed a waiter, and ordered the same as he walked over. Heineken on tap. As they both toasted a productive day, Harry pulled the video from his inside pocket, and handed it to a jubilant dinner companion.

"Harry, you're a magician."

"Is that anything like a pettifogger, Josh?"

They both laughed, and the rest of the evening was spent in good companionship and camaraderie.

CHAPTER 18

All vestiges of the evening's warmth and fellowship were erased when Josh viewed the video. The scenes he watched sickened and repulsed him. Beckman had full use of two pale-skinned, young children. One was lashed to a chair, the other facedown on a bed. They were bullied and coerced into unspeakable and obscene acts, all with electrical shocks. Their small, frail bodies subjected to violations that were discernibly well planned. The audio augmented the torture, fear, and pain.

This was not sexual promiscuity, or even just child molestation—this was naked evil prancing and dancing before him, malevolent self-gratification straight from hell. Where was God? And when the boys swooned, they were unmercifully brought back by smelling salts and made to endure it again. Beckman's usual sickly, sallow complexion took on a rosy glow as he bequeathed this cruel and inhumane legacy to these two children. Bile roiled Josh's usually strong stomach. He needed a cool cloth to relieve the need to throw up.

"The sick fucker needs to die." The words came to him quickly and unashamedly. Vermin like Beckman surely would not be missed.

Sleep did not come that night, and Josh slipped to his covered terrace to get some air. The bright April night gave no warmth. As he stretched his face to the sky, a cold moon spotted him, immersing him in a chalky, white mantle. Abruptly, a spring shower cleansed the night air, but its suddenness failed to dislodge Josh from the chaise, where he had chosen to gather his thoughts with a large glass filled with copious amounts of brandy. He watched, mesmerized in jaded wonder, as a green rain fell. Slowly, the night of the city cloistered him in a robe of unreal peace.

He awoke to the morning chill with dampness and ache in all parts of his body, as he fumbled to the kitchen to fulfill his first desire of the day. Coffee, hot coffee, and lots of it. Midlife moans turned to murmurs when the steaming brew touched his blue lips.

"Ahh, God's in his heaven and all's right with the world...well, almost." The events of the evening came vividly back to life, and the eruption of anger and hate warmed his numb body.

Propelled by a hot shower, gallons of black coffee, and a singleness of purpose, Josh directed all venom within toward a positive design. He picked up the video and shoved it in his briefcase, again feeling revulsion permeate his body when he touched it. Then, at that most unseemly moment of disgust and revenge, the image of a small, goofy Irish setter named Gerti took form in his mind. It made him smile. He missed the old dog. On occasions such as these, when times became out of control and frenetic, he found sanctuary and composure in her unquestionable love and loyalty. Life became easier after she had to be put down last year, but at this moment he would put up with all the shedding, slobbering, and bad breath to have her back. It wasn't so bad. Even when Josh could not perform his doggie duties, he always enlisted the help of Mrs. O'Hara, a retired widow who lived in the same building.

Strange he should think of that dog now. Maybe it was because she seemed to listen so attentively, or so it seemed with her large, brown eyes looking up at him. Now, all his railings fell unappreciated off silent walls.

"Man!" Josh thought. "You've been living by yourself too long."

Oddly, though, thoughts of the old dog had a calming effect on him, and that was what he needed. Calm. Calm to deal with Beckman, an issue he was now quite frankly unsure how to handle. He was ten minutes from the office, and the day had begun. Gentle thoughts of Gerti played in his mind as he shut the door behind him, orchestrating Beckman's downfall.

CHAPTER 19

Monday morning at the offices of Garth Avery and Zoe Erskine, two incoming calls rang within minutes of each other. The one for Zoe was from Josh Lawton, and the one for Garth from Mayor Harris, both requesting meetings.

Josh asked that Zoe see him about noon, to which she reluctantly agreed because of the urgency of the request. Garth was summoned to the mayor's office at his earliest convenience, and responded that he would be there in an hour. After the puzzling phone conversations, Garth and Zoe agreed that whatever the day would bring, it would have a devastating effect on the downtown project. Garth again cautioned Zoe about this Josh character, reminding her again that they knew nothing about him and he was Beckman's guy. Zoe caught herself again. Garth was right; she had only the dinner that night as her barometer, and first impressions could be deceiving. Their hopes for the fulfillment of her father's dream again began to dwindle.

When he arrived for his meeting, Garth was immediately ushered into the mayor's inner chambers. It seemed that everyone had been put on alert for his arrival. When the mayor extended his hand with what appeared to be great warmth and genuine friendliness, the red flag of suspicion flagrantly unfurled in Josh's demeanor. He extended his hand coldly.

"Good to see you again, Mr. Avery," Harris said, beaming. "I know you are wondering why I've asked for this meeting."

"No," Garth thought, "I'm here because I liked your coffee and two-faced, blood-sucking smile."

"Please," the mayor continued, "sit down."

Josh's response to this red-carpet welcome was little more than a half smile and a nod. Garth sat, but in an unrelaxed state.

"I wanted to let you know, Mr. Avery, that I have gone over the plans of Mayor Hanks and Mr. Erskine in detail. After review, the city council and I agree that it would be in the best interests of the city and the taxpayers if you and your associates would continue in the same vein as you did before their deaths. The necessary paperwork is being prepared as we speak. My office has taken the liberty to contact the utility companies—water, gas, sewage, and electric— for any and all needed permits, and the marking of new, old, and ongoing utility lines in progress. All you need do is say the word."

That was it—short, sweet, and to the point. The barricade to three long years of planning, begging, and sweating for this project was removed with a five-minute meeting. Garth was dumbfounded, and speechless. The momentary silence was broken as the mayor's secretary extended a large, brown accordion envelope containing the blessings of the city. Regardless of his dislike, Garth grasped Mayor Harris's hand with gratitude. Harris returned his warmth with a crocodile smile.

When Garth had left, Mayor Harris slumped down in his seat of power, with the look of a man who had just lost a ten-pound trout. As he gazed about his large office, he just hoped the powers that be were listening.

Elated, Garth walked the streets, digesting what the past half hour had meant to him, Zoe, and all the others. Perplexed, he gave some thought to why the mayor had changed his mind, and came up empty. Whatever the reason for his change of heart, it was unimportant. It was like Riza had always said, he thought—"Have faith, my friend, and Allah will provide."

Garth would never know, how much scorpions, black eyes, and Riza had in common with Allah in that sentence. Riza had received news that his friend Garth had left the courthouse with a smile on his face and the pace of a man who had accomplished a mission. Riza smiled broadly. The words "well done" fell from his lips to all within the soothing command of his voice.

CHAPTER 20

Zoe made arrangements to meet Josh at the wiener vender on the corner where Josh's building was located. Seeing her coming, Josh rushed up to her, wrapped his arm around her waist, and kissed her on the forehead. This greeting was uncomfortably enjoyed.

"Your obvious good humor makes me hesitant about this meeting," she said, still very much aware this man was her opponent. "However, your choice of cuisine is excellent." They both ordered bratwursts with the works.

"What I have to say will have to do for dessert," Josh said.

"All right, give," she said. "What's this all about?"

Josh looked directly into her pretty blue eyes, grinned from ear to ear, and told her triumphantly that she would not have Nelson Randolph Beckman to contend with any longer concerning her project. Her face lit up like sunlight bursting through clouds—

first slightly, then with increased intensity. After a few slight stutters of "who," "what," "where," and "how"— and Josh's refusal to answer any questions— Zoe reluctantly dropped her curious inquisition and accepted this gift with grateful humility.

"I will respect your loyalty," she conceded. Then as she thought about it, she realized loyalty intimated love or caring, and she had neither for this man. She decided to consider this subject still a matter of professional ethics. "Here's to professional ethics," she continued. "Now, can we celebrate this obstacle being removed from the project with some wicked dessert? I'm still hungry."

A block away was one of the finest European pastry shops in the city. The sun shone warm and inviting, despite a chill in the air too small to keep them from outside seating. Both ordered the "special" coffee black. The waiter returned with something decadently delicious, with chocolate, rum, currants, and hard sauce, with a bit of real whipped cream on top. Zoe rarely celebrated good news with such spurious disregard of caloric intake, but today was different. She was having a grand time, calories be damned!

Her momentary euphoria over Beckman eclipsed the specter of the mayor, which struck her halfway through her Jamaican Delight. The thought registered on her face in such a way that Josh instantly knew something disturbing had crossed her mind.

"What is it?" he asked.

"The mayor."

Josh wondered how the mayor played into Zoe's plans. Josh was under the impression that all that was needed was Harris's cooperation on all plans and paperwork. That's why Beckman needed something on him, to prevent Harris from signing the final documents. "Why is the mayor a problem for you?" Josh quizzed.

"Extortion, in a word," she said. "Harris has intimated a payoff, a big one, to get this thing off the ground. He insists the public trust would be violated if all taxes on the land and buildings aren't cleared off the books. Everything is on hold until this thing is resolved. Garth and I are out of money. Can't go forward, can't go back. Beckman was only half of it."

"Holy shit," Josh thought, "the son of a bitch is playing both ends." The outcome of this scenario depended on two videos Josh had secured in his wall safe at his office. Essentially, Zoe noted Harris was doing to Garth what Josh had planned to do to Harris.

"You know, bribery, extortion, collusion, blackmail," she said. "Take your pick, counselor, it's all about the same." She again was reminded of the unsavory circumstances Josh and Beckman were embroiled in back at the old elementary school. "Garth is meeting with the mayor today," Zoe added.

"My lady, have no fear, the mayor will not be a problem. Just put your mind at ease. In fact, you will not be going back to your office. You and I are taking the afternoon off."

Unsure of a happy outcome, Zoe took this man at his word. She trusted him, and more and more, she was attracted to him. Garth's words echoed in her ears, "Be careful, we don't know this guy." He was right. Trust but verify, as President Reagan used to say.

Interrupting her musing, Josh's cajoled her, "Come, my lady, we're going to see the wonders of the world. Within New York City, of course."

The rest of the afternoon, they toured the Metropolitan, the Guggenheim and Rockefeller Center, fed the pigeons, and rode in the park. Josh was relentless with his charm, and Zoe was radiant being on the receiving end of his chivalrous prattle. Pure old-world charm and manner. She lost control somewhere between Rockefeller Center and the carriage ride. It was the kiss—an innocent kiss between two people reveling in the day and the pure joy of living. When the day had ended, and she was reluctantly escorted to her apartment, she felt his strong hand clasp her own, and felt his warm lips and breath on her cheek.

Feeling silly, she hurried from the lobby to the small, flashing red arrow pointing up on the elevator. It was six-thirty; the entire day had evaporated. She entered her apartment and headed for the solace of a warm bath. It was there she managed to sort out troublesome thoughts. By eight, she heard from Garth.

"Say, Ms. Gadabout, where have you been all afternoon? Did you get my message?"

"No. No, Garth, I didn't." She had failed to check the voicemail on her arrival.

"Well I've got the best news since Christmas. Look, I'm still at the office. Do you want to eat in tonight?"

"Yes, Garth. I just got out of the bath and I'm really too tired to go out. Chinese sound okay?"

"Wonderful. See you in about thirty minutes, and I'll tell you my news. Love you." And he hung up.

When Garth came through the door, she rushed to him and hugged him tightly, severely crushing the little, wire-handled cardboard boxes filled with Chinese goodies.

"Whoa, hold on. I better bring Chinese every night if it means a greeting like this." Garth good-naturedly tried to maintain control of all the bags he held, and would have lost the battle if not for Zoe catching a couple hurtling to the floor. Most importantly, she saved the two bottles of plum wine Garth had brought for celebration. They scurried to the kitchen and popped a bottle. Within minutes, there were opened boxes of moo-go-gai-pan, sweet-and-sour pork, emperor's chicken, crab Rangoon, pot stickers, shrimp with snow peas, and straw mushrooms. Enough for six Chinese New Years.

This simple take-out meal became a celebration of the end of bad luck and bad tidings, as Garth related the events of the day, and Zoe in turn told Garth of her day with Josh Lawton.

"Did Lawton tell you why or how? I have no idea why Harris handed me the permits, or why he made his commitment to be of service in any way he could."

"Not a peep," she replied. "At lunch, I was only told that Beckman would no longer be a problem.

He seemed genuinely surprised that the mayor had asked for a bribe in order to continue the project. We spent the rest of the day goldbricking. He seemed as if he had a weight lifted from him too."

"It's your charms, woman! No man can resist you." Garth playfully reached over an order of kung-pao chicken and planted a kiss on her nose.

"Is that the best you can do?" she complained. She wriggled her toes up his pant leg and fed him a mouthful of shrimp and snow peas.

"Well, I don't know, so much depends on motivation," he teased.

Garth was a big man with work-defined muscles. She loved to run her hands over his firm stomach, and curled the hair on his solid chest. Moving slowly toward him, she straddled him on the high stool, offering him a sip of her wine. She licked the sweet liquid from the corner of his lips, and continued down to the nape of his neck. Massaging his temples, Zoe stared languidly into his blue-hazed eyes. The open-collared, button-down oxford was slowly removed, and then she allowed her silk robe to fall carelessly to the floor.

"I'm getting motivated," he murmured. No need to explain; she already knew.

She pressed her breast to his, and brushed her lips across his cheek, whispering naughty promises. Raising her legs, she squeezed them tightly around him and drew him near. Standing tall and grasping her securely behind him, he took her to the bed and laid her gently against the pillows. Removing his trousers, he stood before her, deliciously tormenting.

She loved this man with all her being and now, as always, she felt supreme love overcome her as they both became one. He kissed her brow and mouth, lingering at her throat, then followed his desire to her small, round belly, where he dallied with soft caresses. Kissing, cajoling and teasing, he pressed on and down until she could no longer bear the sweet anguish.

By the end of the evening of lovemaking with Garth, Zoe wondered what she foolishly could have been thinking that afternoon.

CHAPTER 21

"I'm telling you, Zoe, I didn't do a thing," Josh repeated, as Zoe thanked him again for taking care of Harris and allowing the permits to be released.

"Garth appreciates everything you've done too. He's been on the phone all morning with the subs and contractors, giving them the green light..."

"Zoe, slow down," Josh begged. "Listen to me, this is a coincidence. I had nothing to do with it. Nothing! Whatever changed Harris's mind, it did not come from me."

"All right, you play coy, Josh, but whoever or whatever, we couldn't be happier. Allow me at least to be grateful."

Josh gave up; there was too much elation and emotion for her to be convinced otherwise today. He would clear it up at some other time. They both said goodbye and returned to a busy schedule.

Ms. Potter's fingers had been busy all morning, corralling all principles in this project. Garth had been coordinating and setting up meetings at the site to get the ball rolling. Zoe had called Father Fitzhugh, advising him that the children's center was not just a dream anymore, and they were one step closer to making it a reality. John Calhern, Ms. Rachel Stone—all were notified that groundbreaking would take place in the coming weeks. Ms. Potter took particular pleasure in calling Klaus. The gift of chocolates had initiated a welcome friendship. Ms. Potter had been a widow for fifteen years, and she had been sorely lacking in companionship.

The office was bustling with activity. Plans, drawings, budgets, and forecasts were spread on the teakwood conference table, ready to be gone over, checked, and re-checked by the onslaught of people who made their way to the office to negotiate and appropriate their time for the months to come. Lunch was several take-out pizzas, thrown randomly on the huge table and eaten in a catch-as-catch-can fashion amid the sea of paperwork and discussion. After months of worry and self-imposed business exile, Garth was overwhelmed by target dates, deadlines, quality of services, quotes, vendors, financial statements—in general, business as usual. He loved it!

As he sat at his desk marveling at the difference a day could make, he spied Warren's watch gleaming in its box. He picked it up and held it for moment, silently mouthing the words, "This one's for you." He placed it back in its box, and continued with the work at hand.

The phone rang incessantly, and one of the calls was from Riza. Ms. Potter immediately rang the minister through to Garth.

"Riza!" Garth boomed.

"Congratulations, my friend," Riza offered. "I understand your project is now officially underway."

"Riza," Garth began, "it was the strangest thing. Harris called me into his office yesterday and offered me the permits on a silver platter. It was as if he couldn't do enough for me. I have no idea what got into him. I only know I have an open line of communication and any help from city hall that I could need. It was strange, very strange."

Riza was happy to hear the joy in his friend's voice. "It is as I have always told you, Garth..."

"I know, I know," Garth interrupted, "Allah will provide." They both chuckled.

"Now to work, my friend," Riza continued, "and let me see the renaissance you promised me. I've yet to have a bad investment in you."

"You can be assured," Garth promised. "Will I see you soon?"

"I shall be in the States at the end of the month, I will talk to you then." As he hung up the phone in his palatial surroundings, a knowing smile appeared on his face, and his dark eyes twinkled. He made a mental note to reward his people for a job well done.

While Garth and Zoe were reveling in their own good fortune, Josh Lawton was intent upon improving his; he was about to become a free man. He left word with Beckman's secretary that he would like to see him first thing the next morning. The little video guaranteed a truce for Garth and Zoe. No more interference with their project, not that they needed it anymore. For Josh, it meant his freedom, a trade for the promise he made to his father. His handwritten resignation of services was neatly tucked in his top breast pocket. He hoped this meeting would be brief. Freedom, sweet freedom. Tomorrow, the shackles of Beckman would be gone forever.

RETRIBUTION, COINCIDENCE, KISMET, IRONY

CHAPTER 22

The headline read: **"Teenage Immigrant Held in Murder of New York Developer."**

"A young man of Eastern European descent is being held in connection with the murder of local developer and entrepreneur Nelson R. Beckman. Beckman was found dead Wednesday morning in the bedroom of his Manhattan penthouse. The body was found bound hand and foot, gagged, and strapped to the developer's bed. An extension cord was found wrapped around his throat, plugged into a nearby electrical outlet. The body was naked except for a leather tie wrapped around the genital area and tightly knotted.

"The victim's wife and the Beckmans' maid discovered the body after Mr. Beckman failed to answer his bedroom door. The suspect was identified by several eyewitnesses, and was discovered in an alley a few blocks from the crime scene, along with twin boys reported to be his brothers. The suspect is being held, pending arraignment and trial, while the twins are being held at a juvenile facility.

"Beckman is survived by his wife Estelle, and his mother Elise."

Josh's eyes focused on Beckman's name is disbelief. After routinely picking up his paper as he had done a thousand times before, on this particular morning, time stood still. His purgatorial state of being had been eradicated in one short headline. Suddenly, his life became infinitely more simple.

Life without Beckman. The delicious thought beckoned a smile to his lips, one he quickly suppressed. Josh had never experienced pleasure at the demise of another human being. It bothered him, until a graphic projection appeared on the horizon of his mind, showing two children being sodomized and beaten by this old monster. He instantly reconsidered his initial remorse. How he died didn't even matter. Hell, he wasn't just pleased the bastard was dead, he was spiritually uplifted.

"Harry!" Josh exploded into the phone. "I need you again!"

"Ah gee, Josh, I'm flattered, but my dance card is filled today."

"Oh, cut the crap, Harry. Have you seen the morning paper?"

"No, let me get it." They both remained quiet as Harry retrieved his paper from outside his door. "Son of a bitch, the old bastard finally bought the farm." Harry had not seen the tape of Beckman, so he really didn't know that Beckman was more than just a slumlord or a run-of-the-mill pervert.

"The boys, I need you to find out about them. Get the two little ones out of juvenile, and check on the older ones' bail. I'll have all necessary papers available for you when we find out what we need. I want them released into my custody. If INS gets into the act, it gets pretty hairy. Find out who we have to get to get this thing done."

"You know this kid, Josh?"

"The two little ones, I do." The pathetic trio, frightened and gaunt, had been caught on camera huddled close to each other, the older one with protective arms encircling the twins' shoulders.

"All right, Josh. I'll rearrange today and I'll be out of here in fifteen. This may not be easy, you know. This kid iced a pretty big fish."

"Yeah, I know. After I hear from you, I'll be down later to talk to the older one."

Harry was right, this was not just some nameless drunk found in an alley. This was Nelson Randolph Beckman, and Josh was his attorney. The press would be hanging from trees, and following the cops' every move. The prosecuting attorney was going to love this baby; this was the sort of case that made political careers. Sullivan must be licking his chops. All things considered, the young district attorney was a pretty nice guy. Josh had lunch with him a few times and found he wasn't a mindless glory seeker. He just did his job, and did it damn well.

Josh finished his coffee, with a thousand questions yet to be answered. He put them on the back burner for now, and prepared himself for the office. He would not got through this day unscathed; after all, he was Nelson Randolph Beckman's attorney. This was going to be one hell of a day.

Two and a half hours later, Josh received a call from Harry, filling him in on the situation.

"Josh," a weary-sounding Harry breathed into the phone, "these guys don't know any more about these kids than when they brought them in. None of them speaks English, and no one in the precinct can communicate with them. They are working on getting an interpreter now. Not that any of them are saying much. They have no identification, of course, and they're all scared shitless. They are talking about trying the older one as an adult. The two little ones are still over at juvenile."

"Harry, you did make clear that they have an attorney. If they haven't said anything up to this point, don't let them say anything to anyone. I'm on my way with my own interpreter. Until I get there, you claim you are the guardian."

Harry had difficultly reminding Josh that he was only a private detective, not a miracle worker. He had a few friends on the force, but not as much pull as Josh seemed to think.

As usual, Harry got what he wanted in his own self-deprecating way. Claiming to be the boys' guardian, he stopped any further interrogation of the older boy until their attorney showed. "No sense in having anyone's civil rights abused because of ineptitude in the department," he said, a subtle but effective proclamation to stall any further wheel turning until Josh arrived.

*   *   *

On the way to the precinct, Josh picked up Gretchen, an instructor at Berlitz and tops in her field. He was lucky to find her with a slow afternoon ahead of her. She was ready in five minutes. Josh had used her on several occasions with overseas contracts—with Beckman, of course, and with several of his other clients. She had little time for levity—or life, for that matter. She was middle-aged and plain, straight down to the horn-rimmed glasses, and seemed content with the life she had chosen. That fertile mind of hers knew every language from ancient Arabic to Zulu. She might be all business, but Josh knew her to be a loving person. Her big, warm, comforting smile would do the job when she came face to face with the children.

Within minutes, they were at the station and behind closed doors, opening channels of communication with the older boy. Josh had stopped long enough to greet Harry and rush him inside with Gretchen and himself. He instructed Gretchen to let the boy know that they were there to help him, and that Josh knew the man he was accused of killing was an evil man. So many things rambled out of his mouth at one time that Gretchen stopped him mid-sentence and asked him to sit down for a few minutes. He was having an unwanted effect on the boy.

Slowly, almost painfully, she brought the boy around. The dull eyes and stone-faced persona began to crumble. He had only spoken to his brothers briefly before the police separated them, and no one except Gretchen was able to get a hint of response from that cold, unyielding stare. It took several languages and dialects before she saw a small flicker of awareness from the stoic face, but she knew she had to use an Eastern European derivation, trying Slovak and Estonian, then Romanian. Then she could feel and see a faint recognition in the eye of someone thinking of a far-off place known as home. Pressing on in a language the boy seemed to relate to, she made him understand that no harm would come to him and his brothers and that this man Josh was here to help them. Far from trusting, the boy at least seemed to foster a small thread of connection between Gretchen and himself. After revealing to her his name, Lech, this young lad—barely beyond a boy and not quite a man—wept.

"He's had enough, we're getting him out of here," Josh interrupted. He asked that Gretchen stay with the boy while he and Harry paid the bail and gathered the other two from juvenile. Within the hour, the boys were all delivered into the hands of Josh Lawton. Before returning Gretchen to her office, he thanked Harry for the extra effort that afternoon. Harry responded with his own "aw shucks" attitude. He told Josh he was heading home for some badly needed shuteye, but said to call if he needed anything.

CHAPTER 23

The car seemed strangely silent after Josh dropped Gretchen back at her office. As she left, she assured him she would be on call if communication became too tough. Gretchen again gave the three boys a reassuring speech, saying all things would be cleared up, and repeating that Josh would take care of them. She left all four in awkward silence. For Lech, promises of this nature were all too familiar, and never to be trusted or believed.

Josh looked at the hapless trio, especially the two little ones. They were confused, gaunt, and— most of all—frightened. At this point, Josh was a little confused himself. The aura of dread and anticipation from the boys was stifling. They scrutinized him feverishly with those large, terror-stricken doe eyes, as if he were a large cat and they were its dinner. Unable to reassure the boys about his intentions, as he saw no change in their behavior, he picked up his cell phone and called his mother.

"Guess who's coming to dinner? I'll see you in an hour or two, with some dinner guests," he added. "I'll explain everything when we get there."

Rachel watched the car pull up with what she considered strange cargo. Puzzlement all but erased her quick smile, though he reached out reassuring arms as she spoke.

"Well, what have we got here?" she said softly, trying to hide her dismay at the sight of the ill-clothed, half-starved children.

"Mother, they can't speak English, and I don't know how long it has been since they've eaten. They have no home."

"Shhh, we'll talk later," she asserted. "I'll take care of the little ones."

Josh took Lech upstairs to the large master bathroom, and was trying to communicate with him when he heard his mother shriek.

"My God! Josh, what is this?"

He arrived in the second bedroom to see his mother's eyes riveted to the body of the twin she had just stripped for a bath. His torso and private areas were covered in big, blue-and-yellow bruises, surrounded by what appeared to be teeth marks. And there was no question that the marks on his buttocks and chest were burns. The boy stood there exposed without a whimper, his head drawn close to his chest.

"Look at the other one, Mother," Josh said.

She unclothed the other twin and found his condition the same. Josh had forgotten that it had been less than a week since he had seen these same children savagely used in unspeakable acts by Beckman. Again, revulsion overwhelmed him.

"Go call Dr. Mellon," his mother thundered. "His number is in the book by the phone. I'm getting these children in a warm bath."

Dr. Mellon was her neighbor three doors down. He and his wife had retired three years ago, and now spent much of their time on charity work and research.

Lech was at the doorway of the second bedroom, watching in horror as his brothers were exposed to more humiliation. However, this time he seemed to understand that these people were here to help, not harm, them. Josh motioned to Lech to help his mother with the two children while he made the call to Dr. Mellon. As Josh descended the stairs, it occurred to him that the police were so caught up in finding Beckman's killer that they had failed to take note of the children's condition.

"When I'm through with them," Josh thought, "Lech will be a national hero for executing a monster." After getting the doctor, and hearing his promise to be right over, Josh returned to find that his mother had handed Lech a towel and made him understand that he was to bathe the same way that she was bathing the twins. Josh led him again to the other bathroom. He turned on the shower, handed him the soap, and made sure he understood what he had to do. While Lech was learning the fundamentals of hygiene, Josh dug up some clothes he kept there for weekends.

By five, they were all showered, bathed, powdered, deodorized, and looking halfway human and respectable. Josh had the foresight to photograph the condition of all the children. Dr. Mellon checked them out, and cursed the animal that inflicted this abuse. This was a kind of assault on the human body that he had seen in only a few cases in his long career.

"They'll be all right, Rachel," Dr. Mellon assured Josh's mother. After hearing briefly about their arrest and interrogation, he wrote out a mild prescription to help the boys rest. Turning to Josh, he noted that a report would have to be made. "I'm sure I'll hear the rest of this when you are ready."

Josh grasped Dr. Mellon's huge paw and thanked him in earnest for his prompt response. He marveled as he always did at how this huge man with his mighty arms and hands was the finest in his field, known for his delicate surgical procedures, and inoperable operations he somehow made operable. He was internationally respected, and Josh was proud to know him.

"I'll call you later, Doc, when this has settled down and we'll talk."

Dr. Mellon scooped up his old and worn relic of a black bag, lumbered down the walk, and folded himself into his shiny, red Corvette.

Silence surrounded Josh as he turned from the door. He surmised the missing foursome had found the kitchen. Peeking around the corner, he found the three boys huddled in a corner, eyeing the fresh fruit overflowing a big, wooden bowl on the large island counter in the center of the kitchen. His mother was too busy pulling food from the refrigerator and pantry to catch the look of unabashed hunger in their eyes.

"Mother," Josh broke into her buzzing about the kitchen. "I know it's against your religion, but what do you say we take these guys down to the Village for a pizza? You can make them chicken soup later."

She turned to him, shaking her finger at him mockingly. "You got a deal, Sport," she shot back.

"We'll take your car; it's bigger," he said, as he picked up three apples and tossed them to the boys. "That ought to hold you till we get there."

Josh had never witnessed such gratitude over such a seemingly small gift. The apples were gone, core and all, before they reached the garage. Opening the rear door of the town car, he beckoned them inside, still facing uncertainty in their eyes.

Rachel turned from behind the wheel and cooed, coaxing the boys with her reassuring smile. They got in reluctantly, unsure again of what lay ahead. Jumping in up front with his mother, Josh suggested she lock all the doors, still concerned that Lech might bolt.

Twilight was near when they reached the Village, and the small township sparkled with tiny lights and soft music reverberating from the taverns. It was more like an Aspen or Vale setting than a typical New England seafaring community. Franco's was a warm neighborhood bar and grill with a family atmosphere. The food was basic, reasonable, and very good. Josh and his mother entered with her holding the little ones' hands, and Josh's arm wrapped casually around Lech's neck and shoulders.

The bedazzled children cautiously surveyed their surroundings, examining every detail with trepidation. Unusual sights and smells overwhelmed their senses, beguiling every instinct that measured fear. They were safe. They knew they were safe. A white-shirted waitress wearing a black bow tie led them to a booth Josh had motioned to just moments before.

"I don't think we'll be needing menus," Josh told the waitress just as she was turning to bring water and menus. "We'll have Franco's Super Duper Godfather salad all around. Roquefort dressing, with bleu cheese sprinkled on top." Josh had made this same request before with the family, surrounded by his nephews, brother, sister, and their spouses. Franco's always spelled enjoyment when the clan got together. "I'll have Heineken on tap and Mother, you want iced tea?"

"Brandy," she broke in, "on the rocks. Tonight, I may have several."

"Bring a bottle of wine," Josh added, "And 7Up for the kids. Better put a rush on that pizza, we've got a hungry lot here."

He grinned at his mother, always the rock, always the patient one, until now. When the waitress was gone and she was satisfied that the children were calm, she demanded an explanation for the bruises — the whya and the how. Josh started from the beginning, telling her everything—Beckman's plan to rob Zoe and Garth of the downtown project already set up with Mayor Hanks, Beckman's dependence on Josh to find something dirty on the new mayor to ensure Beckman's control of the area tabbed for urban renewal, Walt Erskine wanting new schools and manufacturing facilities. How Walt wanted it to be a cleaned-up, self-sustaining industrial park, and Beckman did not want that to happen.

"That's what prompted my visit to you," he continued. "To see what Beckman had on our family, to see if I should continue to do his dirty work."

They stopped their conversation long enough to indulge in the pure joy of watching the children hungrily devour their salads—which they had only done once they understood that it was all right to eat them. They knew how to use knives and forks, but this seemed foreign to them, like something they had not done for a long time.

Josh motioned for them to use their forks, while his mother covered their laps and chests with napkins. They began hesitantly, then ate with gusto. They were not piggish, but certainly ate heartily enough to let Josh and Rachel know the children did indeed have some upbringing at one time. The pizza was unfettered delight, a taste assuredly unknown to the children. Their expressions could only be described as a Kodak moment lost. For the first time since Josh's initial encounter with the children, he saw them smile. The toothsome, wholesome smiles of these children brought tears to the onlooking adults.

"Someone needs to do something for them," Rachel blurted in her motherly, demanding way. "What happens to them, Josh?"

"Nothing for right now. Are you up for them to be your houseguests for the next several days?"

The twinkle in her eye was an unspoken affirmation. "What happened after our last visit, Josh?"

Josh picked up his story where he left off. "I did find some dirt on Mayor Harris, but I didn't want Beckman to pull it off. If Beckman couldn't buy Harris off, he wanted some leverage to crush the downtown project. That's where this becomes interesting. What I had on Harris was on a video. Strictly by chance—by chance!—I caught Beckman briefly on the same video as Harris. I asked my source if he had anything else on the other guy, meaning Beckman.

"Given time, my source came up with another video of Beckman. In the meantime, I get a call from Zoe Erskine telling me that Harris released all the permits and gave them the green light for the project. Zoe started thanking me, thinking I had something to do with the mayor's cooperation. I didn't; something else changed Harris's mind. Of that I have no knowledge, but after receiving the other video of Beckman, I realized the disgusting vileness of this man. That was where I first saw the twins."

Josh nodded toward Lech's brothers, still enjoying their first taste of that smile-maker known as pizza. "Mother, I can't begin to tell you, and wouldn't even try to tell you, the filth and vermin that Beckman embodies."

"Josh..." she stopped him before he could go on. "I have seen many horrific things in my life; you need not protect me from it. I've seen these boys' bodies. If this is by Beckman's hand, I hope Justice is in a very black mood when she condemns him. Is this where Lech comes into the picture?"

"Yes," Josh said, nodding. "I feel he must be responsible for Beckman's murder. But if I have my way, this will never come to trial, given the circumstances. My biggest problem now is the press. Hopefully, it will die down, but I'm not too confident that will happen. Beckman is too big. Too many lives revolved around him, but after I talk to the prosecutor and show him what I have, I think we can make a deal for Lech. For right now, Mother, they are in your hands. When I get back to Manhattan, all hell breaks loose. Half the city of New York, Beckman's widow, and his mother are all waiting to hear from me."

Finishing her drink and motioning toward the children, Rachel beckoned Josh to go. "Come on, we've all had a long day. The children will be fine. They can stay as long as it takes to do whatever it takes. You are staying the night too," she said sternly. "Tomorrow will be soon enough to get back to your rat race. In the meantime, if you're good, you may find some milk and cookies on the counter later tonight." Josh chuckled and called for the tab.

The children, without hesitation, allowed themselves to be swept out the door and corralled in the backseat of the town car. The drive home brought peace to the three confused and tired passengers. Somewhere between Franco's and the welcoming hearth of the Lawtons' home, sleep overtook them. Dr. Mellon's sedatives would not be necessary that night.

CHAPTER 24

Garth leaned back and stretched broadly. He was taking a break. The weeks since Beckman's death had been hectic. Never one to take good fortune for granted, he mused at how swiftly and smoothly the past few days had gone, but remained alert that Murphy's law was a constant in this life. Dozers were running, breakdowns were at a minimum, schedules were met, inventory was on hand, engineers and architects were in harmony, there were no cost overrides to speak of—in short, everything was going smoothly. So why was he so nervous?

When Francis J. Harralday, Warren's faithful counselor for the past thirty years, decided to retire and move to Maine, Garth and Zoe retained the services of Josh Lawton as their corporate attorney. Garth was not as easily convinced as Zoe, given the unsavory nature of Josh's previous clientele. Skeptical by nature, he had a thorough background check performed on Mr. Josh Lawton and his company. Once Harralday's investigators approved of Josh, all corporate papers of the firm of Erskine and Avery were sent to his offices. Harralday said his fond farewells to Garth and Zoe, and happily relocated with his wife and a basset hound named Zeke.

Josh was more than happy to accept the position. Zoe made it clear that it was not out of gratitude, but based on his reputation as a highly rated counselor. Plus, she thought it was good and noble how he was handling the future of the young boy accused of the Beckman murder. Ever since Beckman's death, Josh was eager to help with the downtown project in any way he could, and help with anything else Zoe and Garth needed. Giving generously of his time and money, Josh built a kinship with Garth in a very short time. They were alike in many ways, and worked well together.

Garth knew Josh was hopelessly in love with Zoe, and told him so many times. When Garth and Zoe announced their plans for their wedding shortly before Christmas, Josh deferred good naturedly, saying that the better man had won. He embraced them warmly, and constantly chastised Zoe for not having a sister for him. All in all, they became quite a trio in the weeks since Beckman's demise. Josh had brought in a few more investors, himself included, providing sizable working capital for Garth—more than enough to see him through the next two years and the planned completion date for the project.

He had no more money problems. He was looking forward to finally getting married to Zoe. Everything was rosy. So, why were his palms sweating?

Garth put his elbows on the desk and eased both his palms through his thick, curly hair at the temples. He decided to get another cup of coffee, then decided against it, thinking that must be what was giving him the jitters. He spun around twice in his new, high-backed executive chair, the one Zoe chose for him just for these precise times when he was overtired or edgy. He was grateful for it on a day like this one. He was peering out the window in a half trance when Ms. Potter came dashing in, disturbing the troubled peace he found in his leather cocoon.

"It's Norm," she blurted. "He needs to talk to you right away."

Josh picked up the receiver and heard his foreman bark, "Boss, you'd better get over here right away!"

CHAPTER 25

"**I**'ll bet the old monster's turning over in his grave, spitting maggots," Josh thought, grinning widely as he wrote another sizable check—this time for Dr. Alverez and his clinic, to be held in escrow until completion. From what Garth had told him, that should be soon, as the project was going great guns.

Since Beckman's death, Josh had written many such checks for Erskine Foundation projects. The clinic, daycare, repair work for St. Xavier, training, scholarships, charities. He was giddy, flying high on retribution. How ironic that Beckman left him as executor. Beckman had his father, the senior Lawton, as executor, with a stipulation that Josh would step in as counselor and executor in the event of his father's death or incapacitation.

True to form, Beckman had left his wife a paltry allowance per month, considering his vast fortune and assets. Julie was a pathetic thing. She was old beyond her years, beaten, cowed, and unable to say "boo" to anyone. Beckman had done this to her. Josh remembered her as a radiant young woman at their wedding fifteen years earlier, when Beckman wanted to take her under his wing. Josh was convinced that she genuinely cared for Beckman in a fatherly, protective kind of way. She happily signed a prenuptial agreement. Over the years, he saw her at social functions and business affairs, and in that time saw the light in that young woman flicker and die.

There she sat at the reading of the will—stoic, quiet, immovable. There wasn't a trace of emotion to be found in this solemn, black-clad figure. She sat motionless as Josh droned on about Beckman's assets and how he wanted them distributed. The house Julie lived in was not even her own. Beckman had placed it in a life estate, to be handled by counsel. Everything was in Josh's control—Beckman's companies, his real-estate holdings, his stock portfolio, even the small radio station he picked up six months before at Josh's suggestion. Josh delighted in the irony that Beckman's fortune was benefiting his former rival's charitable and corporate affairs.

Within six weeks of the reading of the will, Josh met with myriad white-faced presidents, vice presidents, and assistant vice presidents of various companies. Half of them were now out on their ear. He had handled Beckman's affairs long enough to know who he liked and who he didn't. Beckman was a miserable taskmaster, and most of his hired CEOs were of the same ilk. Changes Josh made were welcomed with enthusiasm, including employees' profit sharing, new insurance policies, and flexible working hours for longtime employees and new mothers. Offices were buzzing. Walls were painted. Dingy working areas were revived and decorated with new furnishings and paintings. Music filled the halls. There was a new respect from all the employees. Memos flew from office to office.

It was amazing what could happen in a few weeks, given the right motivation. Josh knew he would see an increase in productivity in all of Beckman's holdings. Beckman hated happiness. If only he could see the smiles on all his employee's faces. He would hate it, and Josh reveled in the thought.

He also visited Beckman's mother, Estelle. He never had reason to dislike her, except that she bore the likeness of her son. She was a stately old woman, still in complete control of her faculties and most of her physical being. She needed only the use of a beautifully carved, ebony walking stick to propel her around her vast home. When Josh remarked about its uniqueness and elegant design, she explained her dislike of those horribly ugly, three-pronged steel canes. She was quick witted and competent, living in sleek and tasteful surroundings, odd for an elderly woman who had just offered him tea in her sitting room.

As a courtesy, Josh brought her up to date on the day-to-day happenings of the business, still very much aware that she was a major stockholder in all of them. Josh found that all the changes he had made met with her approval. It was something he didn't really need, but he nonetheless found it had a comforting effect on him. He liked the old woman. Throughout their discussions, through veiled innuendo, he got the feeling that the elder Mrs. Beckman did not always approve of her son's behavior. Could she possibly know the sub-human life form that emerged from her womb? Josh could only speculate. The media circus that had grown around Beckman's death was showing no signs of relief, but Josh and Mrs. Beckman deftly averted any conversation concerning her son and the bizarre circumstances of his death.

Estelle Beckman's extremely gracious manner and sincere interest in the progress of the business prompted Josh to initiate a somewhat regular meeting with her. They would meet on a quarterly basis to discuss the happenings at the various stockholders meetings, and he would update her on any changes and improvements concerning the business. She delighted in the thought that she still had somewhat of a position, and that this young man would consider her views of any value. When her son was alive, she heard little about anything concerning the state of the corporation.

She was wealthy in her own right, with a fortune borne of her husband's ill-gotten gain during the war. In her youth, she had preferred to turn a blind eye to her husband, and to her young son's quest for wealth. She was well kept and pampered, the recipient of expensive clothes and trappings, and a jewel collection to rival any high-ranking Gestapo officer's wife. Little thought was given as to how these things were acquired. In the haunting years that followed, Estelle Beckman gave pause to many things she had overlooked in her youth. When she and her son arrived in New York minus her husband, shortly before the war ended, the accumulated wealth of the family started the Beckman financial empire. It would seem, as many have noted, that the past is inextricably tied to the future. Old ghosts and new hopes emerged from uncanny and unsavory alliances with past and present.

Now the pendulum was swinging for purer motives. Beckman surely would not find a place in heaven, but the legacy he left was heaven sent. It would be put to positive use; Josh would see to that. The twins, Lech, and many more like them would become Beckman's benefactors.

Josh rose and extended his hand to the frail lady he had just now begun to know. Josh knew she would approve of the plans he had for the Beckman fortune. Unspoken words made Josh realize that Beckman had caused this woman a great deal of pain also. In her recessed thoughts, her son's death had removed a great burden from her own regrettable life. He was her son; she had no choice but to love him. All anxieties for her son were now buried with the rest of her torments.

When Josh excused himself, indicating he knew the way out, Estelle asked if he might check on Julie. Estelle had not spoken to her since the reading of the will. They were not close, but the old woman did show concern for her—another indication that she knew her son more than she was willing to admit. Assuring her that this was part of his plans for the day, Josh left her with her thoughts.

CHAPTER 26

Julie answered the door. She had given the staff the day off, something she was fond of doing these past few weeks. She wanted to be alone. Her face ran the gamut from surprise to a look of "oh no, not you again." Sweetly but begrudgingly, she let Josh in. Julie led him into the living room with twelve-foot ceilings and motioned for him to sit down in an intricately ornate, heavy damask chair. The room was decorated in gold and white. Thick, gold-damask drapes hung in billows over thick, white carpeting. There were mirrors, candelabrum, and chandeliers everywhere. Josh had been here many times, but he never remembered it being quite so ostentatious. Beautiful, but just too much.

His silent critique of the interior design was interrupted by Julie's offer of something to drink. He declined, but she walked behind a gold filigree bar and topped off an already half-filled glass of wine. Josh knew this woman was not given to drink, but death, stress, and the unknown had brought many to an alcoholic well. She was dressed simply, in a pair of lounging pajamas, and her face was clean but haggard. It looked as if she had been crying. Her hair was neatly tied back, and her feet were bare. Inwardly, this was a mark of defiance, as Beckman tore into her unmercifully if he ever caught her barefoot. She waited for Josh to speak.

"Forgive me if I'm being forward," he began. It sounded trite and rehearsed, but he was unsure how to handle this hapless creature. He began again, and then decided he would have that drink. He got up, walked to the bar and got his own drink, then started. "Look, you are a young, very attractive woman."

She looked at him, puzzled.

"First, we are sending you away on a cruise for two to three weeks," Josh continued. "Then when you come back all rested and relaxed, I think we're going to have an auction, proceeds to go to Julie Beckman. Aren't you a bit tired of Old Louie?" he asked, glancing around at all the priceless antiques. "Then, I'm selling the house to you for a dollar. How are you at decorating? I'm doing this on one condition—that when you return and get this museum turned into a home, you are prepared to go to work. Beckman Enterprises recently picked up a small radio station, which desperately needs someone to run it."

"But, I don't know anything about anything," she choked and blurted.

"You'll learn Julie, you'll learn. We both will. Now I have to go. You get packed; you have lots to do. Your charges are still open, and you won't have to worry about paying for them."

The old slug had left her a monthly allowance barely above poverty level. A small, childlike glimmer of hope danced across her face. It was contained and muted, but it was there. When Josh opened the door to leave, Julie sheepishly reached up and hugged him, tears flowing unashamedly. There was still beauty there. Beckman's untimely death might allow it to shine again.

CHAPTER 27

Well, it wasn't the first body that had ever been dug up in New York, and it probably wouldn't be the last, but it was a first for Norm. It scared the hell out of him. He'd been digging up, poking around, and tearing down old buildings for the past twenty-five years, and nothing like this had ever happened to him. It unnerved him.

By the time Garth got there, Norm had regained his composure. Darting from the construction trailer, Norm opened the car door before Garth had a chance to open it himself.

"Over here!" Norm motioned in the direction where the old James Buchanan School still partially stood.

Following after Norm at a half trot, Garth stood atop a small hill of dirt. "Christ Almighty," he said. "What the hell is this?"

He stood there, arms akimbo, staring down and evaluating the situation. A skull lay ghoulishly open-mouthed, and a skeletal arm reached skyward. Both were strikingly white against the mounds of brown dirt and brick. Remnants of a red bandana appeared to be looped around the skull through the open mouth, and knotted at the back.

"Have you called the police, Norm?"

"No, Boss. I just called you."

"Go do it."

Norm headed back to the construction trailer to phone the cops. While Norm found this occasion unnerving, Garth found it more of a nuisance, one giant pain in the butt. What was this going to cost him in time, money, and aggravation?

While Norm was phoning the police from the trailer, Garth was making his own report with his cellular, only he was calling Josh. When Josh took the call, he heard the same words Garth had heard from Norm only thirty minutes before. Garth did not go into detail, but waited for Josh to get to the site. By that time, the small hillside was roped off with yellow tape, and a dozen police were checking the area. Josh scurried up the hill in time to see Norm questioned by one of New York's finest, Sgt. Frank DeLuca.

The crew continued using the dozer to gently unearth the remains, while Garth signaled directions to Norm from the front of the bucket. It did not take a forensics expert to see that the skeleton was not that of an adult. The skeletal remains were small, without a trace of clothing save for the red bandana. Unexpected as this find was for Norm, he was about to become an old hand at unearthing graves.

For as he gently lifted the remains from the earth, another white fragment of human bone was discovered. Within the course of several hours, the crew had unearthed sixteen more bodies, all skeletal. None had any trace of clothing, except for pieces of what appeared to be red bandanas, another continuity in this ghastly unearthing.

DeLuca brought in teams of specialists throughout the night, and they set up temporary lighting and labs. Another tent was set up as a gathering place for police to converse, drink coffee, and argue. By this time, reporters and onlookers had made their way to the scene, and set up camp and vigils. Norm and Garth were questioned, then dismissed for the work at hand. Norm and the rest of the crew were sent home with instructions from Garth to phone in and see where this mess was at by morning.

By sunset, Zoe had made it to the site. She had spent the day house hunting in Connecticut. The wedding was four months away, and both she and Garth were ready to trade apartment living for suburbia. Between the shopping, planning, and real-estate agents, she had not been as involved with the project as before. Quivering, red rays of the setting sun outlined myriad police cars, step vans, and ambulances parked on the site, while dozens of white-coated, rubber-gloved individuals interacted with each other as Zoe drove slowly through this surreal scene. Regular police issue surrounded the place, keeping onlookers and gawkers at bay.

When she approached Garth and Josh, they were talking to two plainclothes, Lieutenants Grimes and Mulroney. Wide eyed and baffled, she looked to Garth and Josh for explanation. They finished their small talk with the lieutenants, directed their attention to Zoe, and guided her toward the construction trailer. Within minutes, the grisly story was told. Zoe's reaction, like Garth's, seemed to focus on what this meant to the project.

"To be honest, I'm not sure." Josh had told Garth the same thing only moments ago. Josh was a corporate and tax attorney, so this situation was new territory for him.

They continued to watch the scene unfold from the trailer window, while the crowd grew outside. By this time, more press was on the scene, accompanied by all its trappings. Random, man-on-the-street interviews were conducted with members of the continually growing crowd. Police continued their vigil and peacekeeping, refusing to give interviews.

Garth, Zoe, and Josh ordered pizza from Tiny's across the street, which was getting a ton of unexpected business. The place was overflowing into the street. Tiny himself delivered the pizza and cold beer. He sat down with the three for a moment to take a breather, but refused a beer. Then he trotted back to the circus that used to be his restaurant.

They kept vigil well into the night, chatting, eating, and drinking. About ten, Garth received a call from Riza, who always seemed to know when an ill wind blew in his direction. Happy to hear from him,

Garth relayed the story to Riza. He added he was not sure what this meant as far as work in progress, and that he would know more when the police were finished.

"Keep heart my friend!" Riza cooed into the phone. "This too shall pass."

Garth giggled, thanks to a slight buzz the Budweiser provided. "I know, I know, Allah's gonna take care of this too."

"Oh ye of little faith, my friend," Riza chastised, tongue in cheek. "We shall see."

Riza hung up, and made one more brief call before retiring.

* * *

It was midnight when Mayor Harris was awakened, by what he did not know. His wife slept soundly beside him, as an unseen hand seemed to prompt him to the living room downstairs.

On the table, under a light he had not left on when he went to bed, there was a familiar, heavy, gray paper with bold script. He had received a paper like this only once before, when his wife had gone to her mother's unexpectedly. This one simply said, "Do not stop the progress of Garth Avery's project." Beside the note was a grey-suede jewelry box. When he opened it, Mayor Harris's complexion went white, a considerable feat given his skin color.

The box contained a dead scorpion.

CHAPTER 28

Josh could not get the grim discovery of that afternoon out of his mind. It meant nothing to him, other than a setback for Garth and Zoe. Still, something kept gnawing at him, trying to crawl out of the recesses of his mind. He lay awake, unable to coerce peace or sleep since he left Garth and Zoe at the construction site.

He thought of how many times he met Beckman there at ungodly hours of the night—the cloak and dagger, the routine secrecy, the need to meet under cover of darkness. It all seemed so foolish to him. The one sure finding the police came up with was that the remains of all the bodies—all seventeen of them— were male adolescents. This struck a chord in Josh's psyche that somehow he could not ignore, considering what he now knew about Beckman, the twins he now had in his mother's protective custody, and the school where Beckman always chose to meet him.

James Buchanan had been abandoned for approximately fifteen years, about the time Josh took over his father's practice. It seemed that, for all his money-making real-estate deals, Beckman had an affinity for that school. He was always interested in what was happening to the downtown area, particularly where the school was located. Only when Warren Erskine began earnestly with his downtown plans did Beckman seem consumed by the need to have this property at all cost. There was a thread there. Josh didn't know exactly what, but he damn sure was going to try and find out.

*   *   *

"Police have estimated the oldest remains date to about thirty years ago..." he began.

"Damnit, Josh," Harry replied groggily through the receiver. "Don't you ever sleep?"

"Can't," Josh retorted. "I need your expert help."

"Yeah, yeah. Look, I'm too tired for apple-polishing. What is it?"

"I need you to do some research on an archeological dig."

"Oh Jesus!" came the moan from the other end.

It was almost five in the morning by the time Josh had explained to Harry everything he wanted done. He wanted him to check all police records, starting thirty years back, concerning all disappearances of children and adolescents. He wanted records for cases solved and unsolved, and also any news items pertaining to the career of Nelson R. Beckman. The hour gave Josh just enough time to drive to Suffolk County for another of his mother's hearty breakfasts and a walk in the garden.

Josh always thought better in the comfort of his home in the country. He hadn't seen the boys or talked to his mother in almost a week. He had been too wrapped up in the dispersal of Beckman's estate, and the unexpected pleasure of full control of the Beckman fortune. As he drove with the radio tuned to the classical station, he wondered how long Beckman had been at this depraved behavior. Perhaps, just perhaps, his younger years had been even more violent, more sickening, and hideous than even anyone watching that video could imagine.

There it was again. The connection, that spider web feeling that those long-buried bones and Beckman's fascination with the school were somehow intertwined. For Zoe and Garth, the bones were a roadblock, a nuisance in the path of progress. For Josh, they were a mystery. The night before, there was a moment of remorse among the threesome when they momentarily contemplated the demise of these remains. The police found several parts—skulls and limbs— separated from the rest of the bodies. Zoe shuddered, thinking briefly of the gruesome end these children must have met, but she and Garth saw the remains as faceless and nameless, without a human connection. To Josh, they had names. Nicky, Peter, and Lech—it could have been them. Was he so off base thinking along those lines? He hoped Harry could come up with some answers.

Entering through the back door with a hearty smile, he demanded eggs and bacon from Rachel. The children were already seated around the big island in the kitchen. Both Nicky and Peter let out squeals when they saw him, greeting him with hugs and milk-mustached kisses. Lech just beamed and embraced him warmly. Rachel did nothing of the kind; she was used to his unannounced visits over the years. She grinned lovingly at her son, and demanded he sit down as she poured him a cup of his favorite Amazon blend.

The boys finished their French toast and melon, and delighted in the arrival of Josh. The change in them over the past six weeks had been nothing less than miraculous. They were children again—warm, curious, and full of laughter. But most of all, they had found solace, security, and trust. Gretchen had arranged for a tutor, and the boys were all coming along quite nicely with their English. The fear and hunger had left their eyes. They communicated openly now, able to speak of the past slowly and deliberately.

Lech acted as spokesman for the little ones, telling of how his family had sent them with men who guaranteed a safe haven for the twins and himself. All were unable to know what lay ahead in the murderous regime of Ceausescu's Romania. The boys tearfully spoke of their mother and father, a shopkeeper and pharmacist serving the town of Ploesti, a mining and oil-drilling community at the foot of the gloomy

Carpathian Mountains. Lech spoke of the harassment of their parents by the political police, and how the central committee labeled them subversives. Their parents sent them away when the visits from the establishment became all too frequent, with the promise they would join the children as soon as possible. Lech was given money for the journey—money that was taken from him as soon as they kissed their parents goodbye. They were treated like animals. Shoved on trains and boats, all to unknown destinations, until they ended up in New York.

Josh listened to all this in disbelief. His mother did not; she knew the story all too well. It was a story she lived fifty years ago. Different place, different time. Nazism was still alive. Perhaps labeled differently, but still alive, still breathing, unable to die because of the nature of man.

The twins had put on weight, and the gray hollowness of their eyes had disappeared. The two little ones were more resilient than Lech. The love and caring Rachel showered on the children worked its magic on herself, Peter, and Nicky. She was always a woman young at heart, but now she positively beamed. Though a woman in her seventies, she took on the appearance and demeanor of a much younger person. Josh welcomed this change, this particular spark he had not seen in his mother since the death of his father. He was thrilled to have her whole again.

Rachel looked to Lech for guidance and advice for the boys' new life. Lech accommodated her, but was slow in coming around. At night, she sometimes heard muffled cries coming from his room. She felt it best not to intrude until one night, after checking on the twins, she heard a high-pitched moan that was far too loud to ignore, coming from Lech's room. She threw open the door and found the young man wide eyed and clutching the bedpost. All pretense and attempts at bravado were gone; he reached out to her and hugged her tightly. Rachel hugged back, and assured him he was not to come to any harm.

That was the beginning of many evenings, when sleep would not come for Lech and he found himself awake late at night. He and Rachel would sit at the big island in the kitchen, drinking hot chocolate or raiding the refrigerator, which was always filled now that the children were there.

On one of those nights, Lech had revealed Beckman's terrible secret to Rachel. Even with his broken and halting English, she understood his confession to the murder and his description of the treatment he and his two brothers suffered. She knew this nightmare would be over for him in time, buried if not forgotten. Lech would get through this. Of course, she informed Josh about all of this. In his own way, Josh had become close to the boy, but not to the extent of his mother.

Josh knew Lech would be exonerated. This confession only solidified what Josh already knew. The grand jury would not even bring it to trial, and District Attorney Sullivan would agree once he became aware of the videos. He would lose, and he would know it. Sullivan was an honest and open prosecutor, so his career and political ambitions would have to be advanced some other way. Luckily, the public and press attention had cooled. There were too many other big-time celebs involved in murder and mayhem. Josh had overestimated the notoriety of Nelson R. Beckman. Football legends and murderous moms seemed to share the spotlight when it came to the public's love of the macabre. Murder was becoming as common as Monday Night Football.

When Josh cleaned his plate and motioned for one more cup of coffee, his mother obliged. As she was pouring, she shooed the children away, explaining that their tutor would be there shortly. They all scrambled upstairs, leaving Josh and his mother in a cloud of giggles.

"Now," Rachel asked, "what is it that's on your mind? You're not up here just for my hash browns."

"Caught every time."

"You bet," she quipped. "Want to take a walk with me to settle this breakfast?"

"Sure."

They quickly cleared the dishes and walked out the back door toward the rock garden just as Ms. Holmes, the children's tutor, drove up. Rachel waved and motioned her inside, indicating the children would be down in a minute.

As they strolled through the rock garden and down toward the small pond, crossing the expansive field in the back, Josh asked his mother about Beckman. Puzzled, she quickly answered, "I thought we went through this."

"No, Mother, not that part of his life. Later, in the States."

"Well, you know he was a despicable man, a liar and cheat."

"I know all that, but I was only closely associated with him after Dad died. What was he like before?"

"You realize that I only know from what your father told me. There were times he would come home furious over Beckman's double-dealings, sleazy liaisons, shady partners, payoffs, and downright blackmail. Anything for the deal. I'm sure you realize all that by now. He loved beautiful things, museum-quality pieces. He was a great patron of the arts, gave lavishly to schools, museums, and homeless shelters in those days..."

Josh picked up on the word "schools."

"Which schools, Mother?"

"Oh, he gave to all of them, but mostly the poorly funded public schools in the worst part of town. Your father wrote monthly checks to one in particular, forever funding its athletics and scholarship funds for the brightest students. As I recall, we attended a function in the school gymnasium honoring him. They treated him like a king. The school never lacked for equipment, biology or chemistry needs, he gave them anything they needed. The school plays looked like Broadway revues. The children loved him, which is ironic now, knowing what we know about him. As for his home life, he treated his mother like royalty, with every respect and kindness. How is she, Josh?

Have you talked to her since the funeral? I rather liked her."

"I have," he replied. "She seemed like a gracious woman."

"I know she was thrilled when Beckman finally married. He did rather late in life, you know,"

"Yes, I know. He also treated his wife like garbage. Mother, do you recall the name of the school?"

"No, no I don't, but I do know it was in the heart of the city."

As they continued to stroll, Rachel spoke of dinner parties they attended with Beckman, purely for business. "His past connections with Germany and his oversea contacts brought great wealth to his firm. Your father always believed him to still be a Nazi at heart. He was rather a health zealot, nuts-and-berries kind of thing, rarely smoked or drank, worked out..."

Rachel continued, but Josh seemed uninterested now. He had honed in on her comments about Beckman and his love for the schools, and was unable to dismiss them. That ominous thread of connection was still there, like a spider spinning a web in no particular direction, hanging precariously at the end. Knowing that just as sure as there was a beginning to this web, there would be an end. A natural fulfillment, culminating in the predestined victim's capture. Josh knew the web was encircling the now-dead Beckman. Only in Hell would Beckman feel retribution, but Josh felt driven to uncover the truth about the bodies. The circle would be complete and the truth would be known, if indeed it was the truth.

Somehow, Josh was certain that Beckman was responsible for these children's deaths. He had to find out. Harry would have some answers.

"Have you heard a word I've said?" Rachel tugged at his sleeve, as they aimlessly walked around the beautifully landscaped grounds.

"Yes I have, Mother, every word. You don't know how much you have helped me. Listen, say goodbye to the boys for me. I'll probably be back next weekend. Maybe you'll have your famous cheesecake for me?" Josh kissed her and quickly walked to his car.

When Josh left, Rachel went inside and turned on the news. She was just in time to hear the local newsman announce, "A grizzly discovery downtown, with unknown graves unearthed at the site of the old James Buchanan School..."

Now she remembered the name of the school where Beckman was honored.

CHAPTER 29

"I'll only be gone a week, maybe two at the most," Garth murmured as he hugged Zoe close to him. The call from Riza came late at night, two days after the discovery of the graves at the job site. A well had blown up close to his capital city, igniting two others. Riza was in fear of an explosive situation getting worse. He wanted Garth to oversee the capping of the wells and give direction to his own engineers.

"It's been awhile since you've been involved in one of these," Zoe cautioned, "but I'm sure you're going to do what you have to do." She knew all too well that it was impossible to buck Garth's stubborn streak once his mind was set.

"Norm will be able to hold down the fort for the next two weeks, and the work schedule is all laid out. Thank God the police did not close down the site."

"I nearly dropped my teeth when Harris called yesterday morning. He's been true to his word. I know he had to speed up the investigation with the police commissioner. Cops packed up their tools of the trade and moved on, giving us a clear playing field."

"Norm knows what to do," Garth said. "Any emergencies or decisions concerning the office that ol' Potter can't handle, you can take care of. I'm only a phone call away. I'm glad this all got cleared up before Riza called. I know I couldn't have concentrated as well, knowing this was all back here hanging fire."

Zoe knew she was beaten, and that any feeble protest she made would just make it more difficult on him. She had been down this road several times before with her father, and now with Garth. She learned long ago from her mother that worry for her father only compromised his ability to do his best at the job that needed to be done. Zoe's mother was a wise and strong woman, supportive in every way, traits Zoe was determined to emulate. Her mother did not believe in whining. Because she died young, when Zoe was only twelve, there wasn't time to really appreciate the character of her mother.

Still, Zoe was reminded many times over the years by her father. His refusal to marry again cemented her notion that, to her father, her mother was irreplaceable. He buried himself in his work, but never so much that he did not have time for Zoe. They had a warm and loving relationship, sprinkled generously with stories of her mother. And now, when Gath spoke of these far-off commitments and oil fires, she found herself reminded of her mother's strength and fiery resolve.

"You go, be careful, and get back," she said. "Norm and I will do just fine taking care of things back here. It's obvious I'm no competition for an oil fire."

She chucked and pulled herself down low in the covers. He dove down after her in playful abandonment. Lovemaking was always extra sweet before he left on a trip.

She dropped him at the airport early the next morning, and found Riza's private Learjet waiting as planned.

Before boarding, Garth called Josh, "Take care of my girl. I'll see you in about two weeks. Anything happens, we have everything in order."

"Nothing is going to happen," Josh reassured him. "Have a good trip, and I'll see you when you get back."

Turning his attention back to Zoe, Garth again assured her he was only a phone call away. Zoe hugged him warmly and watched as he boarded and took off, until the small jet became a tiny, silver spot in the distance. She went back to the office to spend the next few days with Ms. Potter. House hunting would just have to wait.

*   *   *

Garth lay back and relaxed for the next few hours, and only began to stir when his inner clock alerted him that his destination was close at hand. Below, he saw the vast desert. No place on Earth affected him quite the same, except the great oceans. The desert evoked an emotional roller coaster of empowerment and humility. One moment of invincibility as you gazed at it, but one moment beyond could bring you to your knees in humble supplication.

Seeing it again brought back bittersweet memories of his days there with Warren. He missed this place. This time, he felt older, much older, without the cockiness of the past. Then he saw it, a defiant black fist. Three in a row rose tall, stark, and unmistakable in the distance. He was disturbed by his assessment of the burning wells.

He was told to buckle up, and that they would be landing in a few minutes. The small plane circled, banked slightly, then came down smoothly and landed not too far from where Riza was waiting in a Jeep. This time, he was out of his flowing white robes, and dressed in basic khakis and a duckbill cap. He was still surrounded by his entourage, but was in the driver's seat this time. When the plane hatch was opened and Garth emerged into the damnable heat, he saw Riza jump out to greet him.

"Welcome, welcome," he roared. "Do you see?" Riza pointed in the direction of the black mantle seemingly encircling his city. "You can smell it too."

"Come on, we'll shut her down. My gear will be here shortly. I had Zoe get it out of storage and send it on the next commercial flight. You got enough explosives for me?"

"I think we have all you need," Riza replied. "Anything else, just ask."

"How about a little refresher course? It's been several years since I've handled one of these babies."

"I know, but Allah would not allow me to choose anyone but you."

Garth looked at him and grinned. "Come on, you got any of that coffee that grows hair on your chest?"

Riza wheeled his vintage, prime-condition WWII Jeep toward the palace. Garth looked at Riza, then at the old Jeep, and then at the blazing sun.

"You sure know how to roll out the red carpet for your guest."

"Ah yes, the Range Rover, she is in the garage. This was my father's; you should remember it well. Warren, my father, you, and I rode in it many times."

Indeed, he did remember. Garth enjoyed every mile of the ride back to the palace.

Riza's residence was straight out of Scheherazade, made of gleaming white marble, with minarets and parapets. Riza proudly held onto his history. Western influence played a part only when he felt extreme discomfort due to a lack of modernization. Several houseboys dressed in immaculate white dress saw to Garth's sparse luggage, while Riza summoned food and drink for them. He then gave Garth a short briefing of the situation, including knowledge of a few armed malcontents in the area. Garth was more than surprised.

"Here?"

"Yes, my friend. It seems we still have those among us who would like to see us swallowed up by our neighbors. We cannot have your American soldiers over here every minute to babysit us, now can we? All the wells have doubled security. I feel we have another fanatic strain of our people out there unhappy with our friendship with the United States."

It was times like this that Garth was reminded of the distance, time, and politics between Riza and himself. They had matured over the years, but neither one had ever thought of the outward influences affecting their friendship in their two obviously different worlds.

Garth slowly became aware that his mild misgivings were growing into a nervous apprehension. The years had taken away his edge, and the knowledge of outside complications did nothing to calm his spirit. Garth was showing the signs of a lengthy trip. Understanding this, Riza acknowledged that the past two days had been exhausting for all. He suggested they would all feel more suited to face the complications of the situation after a good night's sleep. Garth quickly agreed. As they separated, Riza suggested they both enlist the help of the powers that be.

"I know Allah will provide, my friend," Garth said, "but in this case, I think I'll put in a direct line my way as well." As Garth's head hit the pillow, the bright Arabian night embraced the comforting prayer of a man afraid. "Dear Lord, please..."

CHAPTER 30

Why had this thing become an obsession with him?

Josh slammed shut the book he was trying to read in bed, trying but unable to coax sleep. He'd heard from his mother earlier in the evening, and she validated what he already knew. Not ten minutes after he left that morning, she heard the news announcing the discovery of the remains at the James Buchanan School. From all indications, the remains were years old. The red bandanas were also a focus of the news report.

"Josh, that was the school I was trying to think of in our conversation this morning. Why were you interested?" his mother pressed.

Josh still wasn't sure he should mention his suspicions to his mother. What earthly good would it do? Beckman was dead, case closed. He continued to dodge her questions, only to make her more adamant in knowing why he asked them.

"Look, Mother, I'll let you know all about this when I sort things out myself."

As if reading his mind, she added another tidbit to her tales about Beckman in his patronage days. "Did you know that Beckman was not much of an outdoorsman, but he sponsored outings and horseback riding for the older boy students? Girls were not included in these outings. I think it was only fourth to eighth grades. All the boys were issued denim jeans, shirts, boots, cowboy hats, and red bandanas. Your father and I were invited to a small ranch near Kingston that Beckman was thinking of purchasing. He wanted your father to see the place, and to see his boys with their riding instructor.

"Your father told him he was crazy, that he was carrying this foundation thing too far and it was becoming a financial drain. Beckman's charitable habits were not working out in the books. I recall seeing all the boys on horseback, riding around the corral, all dressed in the same cowboy uniform. Eventually, Beckman did not buy the place, through your father's persistence in telling him it was a bad deal.

"I do recall that day vividly; the ride back with your father was not a pleasant one. How your father despised Beckman. More than once he threatened to quit, but I knew he never would because of our freedom, and the debt he thought he owed Beckman."

Josh realized now that his mother's mind was working along the same lines as his own. Impatient with her prodding, he lovingly told her he would let her know if anything else came up concerning these coincidences, and that he would be up next week.

After talking to her, Josh grew even more restless, unable to convince himself that this was nothing. And even if it was something, what would it mean now? Who would suffer from this knowledge, and why was he anointed to unravel this mystery? He had enough on his plate, and the pure joy of just having Beckman gone should be satisfaction enough. Plus, it was all circumstantial. There was no proof, just that gnawing suspicion.

Josh knew Beckman killed those children, just as sure as he watched the video, and he knew why Lech had killed him. Execute was more accurate, but the boys were no longer an issue. Their freedom and future were secure. In a grim way, they were lucky. The scars would take time to heal, but they would heal.

What about the other, long-dead children? Parents, some of them surely alive, would like to know about their missing children. Would it bring them peace? Josh did not know. He only knew he could not let go.

As if on cue, the phone rang. It was Harry's strong, slow, affirming voice that indicated to Josh that he might have something.

"See you tomorrow morning, kid. Eight a.m. sharp." Harry seldom told him anything over the phone. For a tough guy, Harry had his own brand of sentiment. Knowing this was personal for Josh and not just about money, Harry worked day and night with contacts from the police department and the newspaper archives until he came up with something on these decades-old murders.

Harry knew it meant a lot to Josh and—knowing him better than Josh ever understood—Harry wanted to help figure this all out. For Josh, and also for those parents who never knew what happened to their children. Nobody knew better than Harry what it was like to have a monkey on their back that would not go away. He hoped the answers he came up with would help.

Harry's reassurance and the lateness of the hour were finally beginning to bring Josh sleep. All the thoughts of Beckman and the children began to drift away. A small voice, as if in a dream, sent Josh to sleep with a thought of a friend far away. He knew he must remember to call Garth the next morning.

* * *

As usual, Josh arrived early. By seven, he had checked the number where Garth could be reached. He marveled at the fact that he had a minister's personal contact number at his disposal. Sometimes he felt he was living a dream. Garth had introduced him to Riza in the spring, and in that encounter he had given offhand advice that Riza found useful. As if by divine command, he assumed the role of advisor to the minster. Josh had to be living in a movie script. Did it get any better than this? A foreign, stiff voice answered, and Josh asked for Garth.

"Well, are you enjoying sunny Kuwait?" he asked.

"Yeah sure," Garth replied. "I'm nursing my 110-degree tan."

"Are things going well for you over there?"

"Today I found out what I'm up against. Tomorrow I pick the crew, then the party begins. You taking care of my girl?"

"Yeah. If you don't get your butt back here, she won't be your girl."

"Fat chance. She always looked at attorneys with a jaded eye. That one's all mine. Besides I'm better looking than you."

Friendly banter aside, Josh asked a favor of Garth, requesting that the crew set aside anything they found at the digging site near the Buchanan School.

"What do you mean? They haven't found any more bodies, Josh, but they always uncover things—old bottles, cans, jugs. Why?"

"I'm not sure why. Clues, I guess. Anything that might concern those remains."

"Well sure, but why are you interested in this?"

"I'll tell you someday."

"Look, tell Norm what you want. I can't cut into time, I've got deadlines. Tell him to pull a couple of guys out to retrieve anything that looks interesting to you, but keep an eye on the clock. Look, I'm going to get my beauty sleep; I've got a big day tomorrow. See you in about a week."

Josh was relieved he had Garth's blessing. The crews might find something. If not, he would at least know he had done all he could. The forensic teams of New York's finest would probably have done better, but Josh hadn't made the connection when they were on site. Besides, Garth did not need the headaches. He was glad the mayor had backed off.

Still on shaky ground with his suspicions, he had yet to reveal his thoughts to anyone. He knew his mother was beginning to draw the same conclusions about Beckman, but today he was going to unload this excess baggage. As Harry walked through the door, Josh proposed a question.

"Harry do you believe in retribution? Dead or alive?"

Harry, nonplussed at such a profound question at such an early hour, answered him quickly and boldly as he poured himself his cup of joe. "Sure do, kid. You pay now, you pay later, but we all pay. Be it God or man the collector."

"Harry, you do have a unique way of clearing out all the cobwebs. Come on, we're taking a ride over to the site. I've got some thoughts I want to run past you."

"Sure thing, kid. You tell me your dreams, I'll tell you mine."

They talked as they manipulated themselves through the crowded streets. Josh never liked talking business in cabs.

"Harry, I know in my gut that Beckman murdered those kids. He had a thing about that school. We'd meet there at odd hours of the night to conduct business. He practically interrogated me on a daily basis as to the activities going on with Erskine, and his bid to get that school and the surrounding area. It didn't strike me then, of course. I thought it was just hate and competitiveness with Erskine, but it didn't subside when Zoe and Garth wanted to continue the project. It's ironic Beckman had a part in my thinking. If he had not been driven to get leverage on Mayor Harris, we never would have seen Beckman on video. This has all been an accident, Harry, a frigging accident! The old monster never expected to be caught. But he's dead, Harry. Dead, the kids too. How do I prove it, and what good would it do?"

"Let's just say it would have a cleansing effect on you, and closure for some parents. Curiosity was getting the better of me too. Detective DeLuca helped go through the police cold-case files and paper archives. We found the names of sixteen children out of one hundred and five who went missing and were never recovered. All white, between the ages of seven and sixteen, during the years 1965 through 1970. These sixteen missing children all had one thing in common—they went to the Buchanan School. They fit the forensics timeline for the bodies recovered. None of these missing boys were itinerants or derelicts. They all came from two-parent, middle-class families.

"There are some parents who still have not given up hope of hearing something. I talked to a couple of them, Josh, and it was something they thought they had put behind them. I did not want to raise their hopes, and I told them my visits were for research purposes."

"Harry, I'm hoping to find something, anything, that might link Beckman to these kids. It's more than a shot in the dark, isn't it? It's probably impossible, but I talked to Garth, and he okayed the guys to set aside anything interesting from the dig. Hell, I feel like Indiana Jones."

"Yeah, me too. Just don't have me riding a horse beside a Nazi tank."

* * *

Norm was at the trailer, and he was expecting Josh. Garth had given him a call to explain the visit. Norm was visibly perturbed and put out, but reluctantly helpful. Garth knew his foreman's temperament, which was why he suspected he had better make the call before Josh's arrival.

"Hell, man!" Norm marveled. "We dig things up all the time, but we've got deadlines to meet. We can't stop and examine everything we turn over. You want me to pull two men to sift through dirt?"

Josh realized how silly this all must sound to someone like Norm.

"We chase kids out of here all the time," Norm continued, "trying to get in here to dig through dirt..."

"Kids!" Josh yelled. "That's it! We need kids!"

Harry and Norm stared at Josh in wonderment. Within a heartbeat, Josh was talking to Zoe on his cell, getting her to call Father Fitzhugh.

"Look, tomorrow is Saturday," Josh said. "You're not working, right?" Norm nodded. "What if we brought kids over to do this for us?"

"Are you crazy, man?" Norm exploded. "The insurance, the liability. They could get hurt, anything could happen."

"Come on, Norm, not with the right supervision. Want to play scoutmaster for a day? I'll take full responsibility for the outing."

Beaten, Norm relented. Josh gratefully shook Norm's hand in stony silence and said he would see him the next morning about nine. Josh did not illicit a smile from Norm. The attorney and gumshoe likened Norm's grumbling to that of a gut-shot bear, an amusing term Harry remembered fondly from his uncle.

At nine the next morning, the site found itself crawling with twenty-five of St. Xavier's munchkins. The enthusiastic children took their task to heart, and none found themselves reluctant to do the job outlined for them. The children, of course, looked upon this as a giant outing, a license to root and get dirty to their heart's content. A giant scavenger hunt was laid before them. It was mostly boys, but a few girls threw their hats in the ring. They were instructed to report anything that looked interesting, or anything they were not able to recognize, and bring them to an appointed meeting place.

By this time, Josh had opened up about his suspicions to both Father Fitzhugh and Zoe. They both listened, dumbfounded. After hearing the story of the twins, and their treatment on the video, Father Fitzhugh did something very un-priestlike. He spat indignantly, like a street fighter, and vowed to Josh that the unholy scum who did this would pay by the hand of God. At times, Father Fitzhugh's priestly trappings gave way to his baser instinct of loathing for some of man's inhumanity to man. He hated bullies, those who preyed on the smaller and weaker. He found himself praying for guidance and understanding when he was faced with a particularly troublesome boy with a chip on his shoulder. Patience and love usually brought many around, but he knew there were some who were truly the devil's own. He prayed for their souls, leaving the more complex judgment for the almighty. For his part, he found forgiveness most difficult when faced with stories of such brutal, sickening behavior.

Without letting Josh continue, as he needed no more convincing, Father Fitzhugh rose. Looming tall as an avenging angel over Josh and Zoe, he announced the children would be ready for their task. He did not even give a thought to the irony that these small, helpless ones may well be the investigating forces who brought accountability to an evil dead man, and peace of mind to Josh. His nights and days were tormented since he saw the video almost three months ago. He needed some closure to this, even if they found nothing. It was the knowing that he had tried that would allow him undisturbed sleep once more.

It was early afternoon when the adults noticed a slowing down of the troops. It was again Tiny's incredible ribs and pizza for all, and that fueled the slagging group to continue their quest. The kids were instructed to separate bottles, cans, and anything that was glass or pottery. Norm was on the big Cat moving dirt, with a grinning nine-year-old on his lap. Norm was usually as grizzled as a day-old beard, but this particular youngster had managed to pierce that granite-faced exterior.

"I've known that man for most of my life, and look at him!" Zoe marveled. "He's smiling!"

And sure enough he was, allowing the carrot-topped kid he had in his lap to operate the levers and steer, much to the chagrin of the others below. Before he knew it, kids were lined up, as if for pony rides in the park. Norm was loving it.

"See, Father," Zoe observed. "I know miracles happen every day. Look at Norm. As a child, I would come to job sites with my father and Norm would be there. He never let anyone near his equipment. He was as cantankerous then as he is now, but he always had cherry cordial chocolates for me when he knew I was coming."

The quest continued until the shadows got long and the children grew tired. And in the end, it was all too simple. A few precious and fine articles were mixed in among the tin cans, bottles, old tires, little-girl barrettes, shoes, quarters, dimes, cigarette lighters, and various sundries. There was a gold watch, covered with dirt but intricately carved with the initials "N.R.B.," an 18-karat-gold cigarette lighter, gold belt buckles, two money clips. Among a dozen pocket knives, four were pearl handled, all bearing the initials "N.R.B." They lay in a neat row, echoing anguish from the past that Josh now found audile, tangible, and very real. He held a smooth, ball-like object with Beckman's initials. It only took seconds to understand it was the top portion of a broken cane. It made Josh cringe to think of what uses Beckman had for it. Dropping it in disgust, he again thanked Father Fitzhugh and the children for their participation, and sent them home.

Norm and Harry left, and the site suddenly took on an eerie, distant, lonely feeling. Zoe and Josh were left standing in the fading daylight, with soft rushes of whirling dust obscuring their view of the setting sun.

"Come on," Josh finally said. "Let's get out of here. I'll walk you to your car."

"I guess you've found your answers," she declared as she started to open her door.

Josh just shook his head, knowing she wanted to help but couldn't. Zoe hugged him warmly and told him to call if he needed anything. Her previous infatuation with Josh had evolved into a deep friendship. As she watched him drive off, her thoughts turned to Garth a continent away. He was due back next week, and she was going to make his homecoming special. A soft smile took hold of her face as she thought of his return.

CHAPTER 31

Her name was Khali. Her large eyes were the color of ripened dates, and her exquisitely chiseled nose and jawline epitomized the signature of her breed. The nose of this delicately carved face nuzzled in Garth's extended hand, indicating immediately that this man was accepted. Khali was Kahalan, one of the five strains of the Arabian. She was the favored one in all of Riza's stables. It had been years since Garth had been riding, and that was in Central Park with Zoe. Not since his earlier visits to the Gulf had he ridden such an animal. After the firestorms and stress of the past week, he was ready for a day of relaxation and celebration for a job well done. So it was that he gladly took the invitation to ride with his old friend.

It was early, as one did not sightsee in the desert in the latter part of the day. Garth marveled at how some things never changed, and never did a saying hold more truth than in the timeless rapture of the desert. Civilization and modernization had tamed it somewhat, but the conquests were small. The respect of a thousand years was obvious. Like the oceans, it had the capacity to minimize your entire life and existence to nothing but a whisper.

Garth gave way to freedom that day, and he and Riza raced as they did in their youth. Unfettered, he thought of nothing concerning construction, deadlines, or work in general. God, he hadn't felt this good in years. He felt the hot desert air, the horse beneath him, and the comfort of Zoe's arms. The winds had blown the acrid smell of the smothered wells away, and the air was renewed. Life was good.

*   *   *

Fate, pure and simple. Not the horse, nor the proficiency of the rider. The accident came suddenly, like the small, swirling sand devils around them. A soft thud and the wrong alignment of the body left Garth in a stunned and immobile position. His mind was clearly seeing himself rise and remount, as if he were dreaming, but his body was not responding.

It was not until Riza was kneeling above him that he realized the predicament he was in. An icy fear enveloped him, and slowly the heat of the surrounding desert turned cold. Garth was scared, more scared than he had ever been in his life. Riza covered him with a small blanket. Time and reality stood still. A blurred Riza was speaking, but Garth lay there unable to decipher the meaning. He swooned, and his memory retreated.

Riza rode as he had never ridden, for his friend's life. They had no cell phones on them, as they had left the bothersome devices behind. Within the hour, every medical device and form of assistance was at Riza's disposal, and skilled paramedics had transported Garth to Kuwait's finest hospital for around-the-clock supervision and monitoring.

News came quickly, but the operative word was "wait." Zoe was contacted shortly after the doctors made their initial diagnosis. Riza reluctantly told her about the events of the past several hours, and informed her his jet would be at her disposal.

Josh would not be dissuaded. After a frantic call from Zoe, he was on that plane with her. Within the next few hours, they had arrived, greeted Riza, and gone to Garth's bedside. The next several hours would take their toll on Garth's friends—and, of course, the most on Zoe. Anyone who had been through such a process knew the waiting could be more terrifying for the people waiting than for the patient. They had heavily sedated Garth, and Zoe would not be able to speak to him until the following day.

The night was long for everyone. Riza and Josh broke away from Zoe, giving her some space, only to pop up every so often to see if she needed anything. Zoe would not leave the hospital, so Josh and the minister stayed with her. Which meant Riza's ever-present bodyguards also had a long night. Most of the time, they stayed silently in the background, unheard and unseen. Sometimes, their presence was remembered when an unsuspecting resident or nurse made their way to this private floor. They were subtle and precise. There would be no disturbances for anyone tonight, unless it was the doctor administering care.

Josh and Riza busied themselves with mundane conversation and walks around the hospital grounds. The night grew long, and they all caught cat naps throughout its long silence. They waited, and they slept. Conversation grew scare. All anticipated the morning light.

The morning broke, hot and glorious, engulfing the whitewashed city. The first plaintive call of the muezzin was heard, high and lonely, wooing the faithful to prayer. Riza disappeared for his own moments of privacy. Zoe awoke with a start, immediately praying to God for Garth's recovery. She approached the nurse on duty, hoping for any positive news, but it was not forthcoming. Morning brightness grew into afternoon shadow, and it was not until late in the afternoon on the second day—when the fifth and final call for prayer to Allah was summoned— that Zoe, Riza, and Josh saw Dr. Rasul greeting them with a wide grin and a fast-approaching gait.

Ignoring Zoe, he spoke directly to Riza, and announced with great gusto that the patient was out of danger. Though the fall had severely traumatized the spinal cord, it was the general consensus of all attending physicians that there was no irreparable damage, provided that the patient remain in somewhat of an inanimate state for an undetermined time.

Garth just needed rest and time to heal his badly bruised neck and spine.

The next face the threesome encountered was that of a very groggy, almost-coherent Garth. He mustered a weak smile when Zoe reached greedily for him, careful not to disturb his position. Catching his breath from her onslaught, he peeked over her shoulder, eyed his two friends and winked. Whether they called him God or Allah, it seemed he could not bring more joy to anyone who was in that room tonight. God and Allah be praised.

CHAPTER 32

The night was intoxicating, as someone so aptly put it. The stars rained down in torrents as Zoe and Garth gazed toward the heavens, so full of laughter and love that the surrounding quiet of the forest echoed with mirth. Recovery had been hard, long, and tedious, but never once did Garth feel he would not regain full use of his legs and all his motor skills. He was strong and he knew it.

After a month in Kuwait with excellent care, Garth asked that he be released to go home. His injuries were bruises and trauma, things he understood. What he did not understand at that point was that time and his inertness were the keys to recovery. The healing process would begin; it was the length of time that frustrated him. Never a man to stay still too long, he was irritated by the bed rest and inability to function at his normal pace, until Zoe and the doctors put things into perspective—Garth would fully recover in time; others in similar circumstance were not so lucky and ended up in wheelchairs.

Garth promised to follow the doctors' orders, agreeing to supervised rehabilitation and promising not to take it upon himself to play doctor. With this promise, he was released into Zoe's care. She took him home and directly to their cabin, now equipped with a hospital bed and a visiting therapist from the nearby village.

*   *   *

This night was special. They had been at the cabin for nearly a month, and this was the first time they had ventured out for a short walk. A very short walk, but a walk!

Garth had a little difficulty with his speech, but now that had completely disappeared. By the end of the second week he was back making wisecracks at Zoe and their occasional visitors. Visitors were allowed, but Zoe made it clear to everyone concerned that Garth was not to be disturbed with anything concerning the project and its progress. Her mandate held fast until the beginning of the third week, when she noticed that not knowing how the downtown project was coming along was doing him more harm than good. When she allowed Norm and Josh to report every three or four days on the status of the project, she found Garth took on a particular glow that she was unable to supply.

By the end of the sixth week, Zoe gave up; she was no match for his pent-up enthusiasm. They made a deal. There would be no plans for a large wedding. They would quietly get married and spend two weeks at sea, where Garth could continue his therapy and focus on complete rehabilitation. Garth happily agreed to this. No sooner had the words been said than Zoe had the bags packed. She helped Garth into his temporary wheelchair, got them into their car, and headed back to the Big Apple—straight to the docks, where they booked a trip on the Star of Norway.

After being quickly and seamlessly checked into their cabin, Garth looked at Zoe, bewildered by the whirlwind transportation from mountain cabin to ship.

"You had this all planned, didn't you?" he said.

"You are all mine for the next two weeks. Then you can go back and play with your project. You are not out from under doctor's care. Yet."

Zoe and Garth were married at sea by the captain, and Garth continued his therapy. The warm sun and waters worked magic. When the two-week therapy cruise came to an end. Garth walked into his office after three months.

He was married to Zoe, he could walk, and the day was beautiful. He was a blessed man.

CHAPTER 33

"Guess what?" Zoe chortled to Josh as he walked into Garth's office. "We're going to be your neighbors."

She was perched on Garth's desk, amid preliminary renovation plans for a house she had found in Suffolk. A bewildered Garth was trying to seem interested, but his mind was elsewhere at the moment. Norm called about fifteen minutes ago, petulant about the bricklayers Garth had engaged. Garth told Norm he would be at the site in twenty minutes, but Zoe had him imprisoned in preliminary architectural renderings.

"Thank God you're here, man!" Garth bellowed. "Rescue me. Norm is threatening to run my brick man over with the dozer.

Garth's good-natured dismissal of Zoe and the drawings did not sway her enthusiasm. She simply scooped up the papers and continued, engaging Josh in her verbal tour of the home and all its amenities.

She took his arm and led him toward the door. Josh looked helplessly over his shoulder toward Garth, who merely shrugged and grinned at him.

"Obviously, these contracts do not have to be signed today," Josh said, taking a shot at freedom.

"No, go." Zoe ushered him out the door in a whirlwind of house talk. Garth immediately followed, hoping Norm wouldn't run *him* over with the dozer for being late.

Josh had no idea he was heading for Suffolk that afternoon, but Zoe felt he had to see the house since he would be drawing up the contract and offer. As usual, the lady always seemed to get her way.

"Call Tiffany," he begged, wanting to tell his ever-faithful secretary that he was taking the day off. Josh knew that day's calendar was not all that full, and he was sure Tiffany and his new assistant, Henry Rath, could handle what little there was. This past year had brought more business than Josh and his two associate lawyers could handle. His need for a new assistant and associate could not be ignored. Henry joined about two months ago, and over that time, proved himself a valuable asset.

Josh had always known his own knowledge of criminal law was restricted, but Henry filled that need in the Lawton firm. Until Beckman's death and the incarceration of the boys, murder was something Josh had never dealt with in his law firm. He knew that were it not for the "Beckman Tapes," Josh would have been in over his head if Beckman's murder had gone to trial.

He was lucky that Sullivan, the hot-dog prosecutor, did not belabor the loss of the case. Josh's initial respect for the young man was heightened, so much so that he offered Sullivan the job before Henry. Sullivan declined, and rightly so, as much would be heard of this young man in the years to come. After seeing the videos and reviewing the connections between Beckman and the school, Sullivan made the Beckman case go away. The headlines and newsworthiness soon faded, and Josh was grateful.

"All right," he said, again focusing his full attention on Zoe. "Let's go see this house you are so crazy about. We'll stop off and see my mother and the boys while we're there."

Zoe felt this was an added treat. Zoe and Garth had met Josh's mother and the boys in June, soon after Josh took over the responsibilities of the Erskine Foundation. Zoe felt Rachel was a delightful woman.

"Wonderful," she chimed in, looking at Josh intently, "Do you think she might have some of those wonderful baked goods on hand?"

"She always does," he responded. "In fact, I'll call ahead, and we'll have a late lunch there. She will love it. I should have set her up in the restaurant business years ago."

His new black Mercedes—compliments of the Beckman Foundation—headed north until it was lost in a sea of October color on the back roads of Suffolk County. Their journey soon brought them to an old Tudor home with massive wood doors and leaded-glass windows. Huge lion-head doorknockers stared somberly down at them. They found the realtor's combination lock open, as Zoe had called the agent earlier. She apologized for not being able to be there, but assured Zoe that the house would be open when they arrived, considering the hefty deposit Zoe had made. Zoe promised all doors would be locked when they left. The giant doors squeaked loudly as they entered.

"Why did I know they would do that?" Josh said in a comical whisper.

Zoe stared at him coldly, chiding him with her eyes. And there it was, cobwebs and all. They found themselves standing in the huge foyer of a house with marble flooring, a winding staircase, massive hand-hewn beams, and a garish cherub-covered chandelier hanging above them.

"You've brought me up here for my opinion?" Josh asked. "You've got to be kidding. Are you sure we're not on an old Abbott and Costello set? I mean, where are the coffins? The rattling bones, the ghostly apparitions—hell, where's Dracula?"

"All right!" she boomed, getting to the point of exasperation with his good-natured humor. "You're worse than Garth. Now stop this nonsense, and really take a look around."

Josh tried to overcome his obvious amusement, because the slight tinge of anger in her face could not be denied. "All right," he said, standing chastened with his head bowed. "Let's see the rest of this gruesome thing."

"Come," she said in a low, breathy voice. "Let me show you to the drawing room."

Raising her arms straight out, walking slowly and deliberately as if in a trance, she guided him through two more large, oak-paneled doors, showing him that she was not totally without humor about the place. She challenged him to look around with an open mind, and then give her his opinion. Josh did just that.

Despite the cobwebs, dust, and obvious disarray and misuse of the old place, the high October sun shone brightly through the beveled and leaded glass windows that reached proudly from floor to ceiling. The light gave the house a hallowed cathedral affect. The hardwood floors softened when awash in sunlight, and the huge, gray-rock fireplace took center stage as the focal point of the entire room. With every movement of the sun, the light was left to its own devices— bouncing off the walls and showcasing the intricate detail of the hand-carved crown molding.

Josh found himself sitting on the huge hearth, actually enjoying the true feel of the room. The vastness of the space was not overwhelming. Indeed, it had a warmth and coziness, a protectiveness that was almost sacrosanct. Sitting down beside him, Zoe saw that he was visibly impressed.

"Isn't it beautiful?" she whispered, gently interrupting Josh's own awestruck feelings for the room. "There are no ghosts here. And if there are, they have guardian angels for roommates."

"You're right," he admitted. "There is a feeling here. A good feeling."

"Come on, let me show you the rest."

Despite its massive appearance, the house was not all that large, about 3,200 square feet. The living room and dining room were also impressive, though they lacked the strangely comforting feeling of the drawing room.

The kitchen, however, was a different story. The most recent owner, a family trust, had not felt the need to renovate. The sink was a deep double bowl made of concrete, and the faucets had exposed copper piping, topped by 1920s-style handles with small porcelain circles that bore the initials for hot and cold. When the water was turned on, the pipes sounded their displeasure. The counter was a real butcher block, which was not so bad, though rather unsanitary. It was the only thing that reeked of any charm. Everything else just reeked. There was very little cabinet space, and the few cabinets it had were old, painted, and ugly. An avocado-green dishwasher was installed randomly some thirty-odd years ago. Worn, red-brick-pattern linoleum framed the whole awful scene. Josh looked at Zoe, who somehow seemed oblivious to all this.

"Zoe?" His voice was one of resignation, and he asked almost reluctantly. "Are you sure you are ready for this handful of headaches? Do you realize what a money pit this is? What about heating and cooling, and a little thing called insulation? Have you checked these windows out?"

"Everything is original, Josh. There is no central air, and the furnace is coal."

"Coal? You've got to be kidding." He found himself repeating this phrase several times throughout the remainder of the tour. "How long has this white elephant been on the market?"

"Almost six years," she said, leading him down the deep, dark stairs to the basement.

"I was right, this *is* a dungeon," he said, zeroing in on the barred door immediately in front of him.

"Don't be silly, that's the wine cellar."

Actually, the area was not that large. Its walls and floors were made of large, gray stones that looked as solid as the day they were set. Over in the corner, more ancient plumbing extruded from what seemed to be the water heater. Not too far from this stood the biggest furnace Josh had ever seen. It overwhelmed the small area where they were standing. His attention, however, seemed directed to the small alcove behind the barred door. Here he felt a history of people who enjoyed the good life.

"Isn't it great?" Zoe broke into his preoccupied examination of the shelves and giant, stone-carved benches. The benches seemed to be afterthoughts of some overzealous stonecutter, who made this charming retreat from what could have been a very boring, but functional, room. "Come on," she goaded, "we still have more to see."

Moving quickly through the kitchen, she pulled him by the sleeve through old, French-style doors located on the far end of the dining room. With this childlike gesture, they were transported through the looking glass. They stood like storybook drawings, gazing at the giant pines and spruce that surrounded this magical glade. Sun fell through voluminous boughs, throwing splinters of sunlight to dance off great polished stones and careening waters. These were natural, spring-fed waters of which some creative gardener or landscape artist took full advantage, leaving this botanical legacy of wonderment.

They viewed all this enchantment from an elongated patio made of quarried slate, colored in hues of gray and blue that spilled down craggy steps onto a carpet of emerald-green ground. Weeds did not seem to exist in this mystical arena. They both stood still in mute appreciation for several minutes, experiencing their Shangri-La surroundings. As if on cue, a spotted fawn emerged from the woods to disturb their reverie.

"I want this place," Zoe whispered. "It's been waiting for me. Come on."

They both retreated to the French doors, and Josh seemed almost dazed.

"I feel like I just fell out of a Disney movie."

"So, what do you think?" Zoe looked blissfully up at him, looking for his approval.

"All right, it's great, but what about the money pit part? What about the roof? Does it leak? I noticed some rather suspicious spots on the ceiling. What about the plumbing and the electric? And the kitchen? I haven't even seen the bathrooms. There are bathrooms, aren't there?"

"Oh, stop fretting. You sound like an old maid aunt. The house is basically sound, and Garth can do anything."

Garth's name brought Josh tumbling back to reality. For the last several hours, he had been caught up in Zoe's excitement. He felt like a kid exploring an old house with his best friend. But Zoe was not his best friend. Over the past year, Garth had taken that role. A loyalty and devotion had developed that neither man had expected. Zoe was more to him; this he could not deny. He watched her ascend the stairs, looking back at him, prompting him to follow. Smiling brightly at her, he shoved aside thoughts and feelings he wished he didn't have to deal with. The tour was almost over, and Josh was thankful.

CHAPTER 34

Beckman's vast fortune and his assets were being put to good use. Josh made sure, however, that Beckman's name was not associated with any good deeds, foundations, or trusts. It was not within Josh's soul to have that name remembered and honored. Still, huge amounts of his money were given to funds to fight child abuse and homelessness, and Josh meticulously monitored them to see that the money was put to good use.

Lech, Nicky, and Peter were set—they had become part of the Lawton family, blending in neatly with the aunts, uncles, and cousins. Josh thought of them as his own and was working on adoption, but his mother's loving care and attention were enough until then. Visits to his mother became more frequent. Trying to be a weekend father was something new to Josh. He liked it.

* * *

It was the second week of October, and Suffolk County's celebrated autumn season did not disappoint in its maddening charm of fall colors. The intoxication of the season brought even the most dedicated couch potato outdoors. The outside air harbored the chill of the winter to come, but the warmth of the autumn sun beckoned a celebration.

Josh and his mother had planned one of their famous barbeques, and the time was ripe for gaiety. Years before, people came from miles to be hosted by the Lawtons. Josh remembered well how, as a child, he and his siblings were part of their parents' hospitality. The Lawton barbeque was almost an annual event, looked forward to by half of Suffolk County. After his father's death, the event waned, as his mother had no heart for hosting such gatherings without her husband.

With the addition of the children, however, the old mansion took on a new life. Even the small stable below the house, where Josh had a pony as a child, enjoyed new life with a welcome addition—a fragile-faced beauty called Khali. After the incident with Garth, Riza was going to put the horse down. Garth would have none of it, and asked for the horse as a gift, to deal with at his pleasure. His pleasure was knowing a friend named Josh who had a stable, and three children who would love Khali.

All in all, Josh's life was taking on a new direction, one as fresh and clean as the October sky on this Sunday. He helped his mother guide and direct all manner of caterers, florists, and a fellow with a

Spanish guitar. The unmistakable clink of horseshoes, and shrieks from volleyball players, echoed throughout the day. Josh bonded with his family, met new neighbors, and renewed old acquaintances with the surrounding community. Harry showed up with Josh's secretary, Tiffany. Father Fitzhugh brought a small busload of kids. John Calhern came bearing gifts of the finest wine. New faces and old came meandering in throughout the day. Dr. Mellon, Norm, many of the investors in Garth's projects who were finally seeing their hopes become a reality. Klaus and Ms. Potter made an appearance, both acting like schoolchildren. The day was a rousing success for all involved.

There was a tinge of sadness, or perhaps envy, when Josh saw Garth and Zoe so happy and so in love.

"Well, hello, Mr. and Mrs. Avery. How are my soon-to-be new neighbors?"

They all embraced warmly and set about idle conversation throughout the day.

"Oh Josh," Zoe offered, "I hope you don't mind. My cousin is in town and will be staying with us for a week. She is thinking of relocating. I invited her to your outing today. I hope that's okay with you."

"Of course, the more the merrier."

"In fact," Zoe interrupted, "there she is now."

Josh turned, and was greeted by a woman with the most beautiful blue eyes he had ever encountered. At her feet, practically tripping over her ears, was an Irish setter puppy.

"Tell me," Josh thought. "Does life get any better than this? We'll see."